Dracula's Women

Ariel Slick

Published by Ariel Slick, 2024.

This is a work of fiction. Similarities to real people, places, or events are entirely coincidental.

DRACULA'S WOMEN

First edition. January 30, 2024.

ISBN: 979-8224774364

Written by Ariel Slick.

Chapter 1

I had this man right where I wanted him.

Jonathan Harker looked so beautiful in the moonlight, fear and desire written equally on his face, his brown eyes huge, glancing around the room, wondering if he were in a dream.

No dream, my sweet pet, but a most stunning nightmare.

I knew what he saw when he looked at us, for we were deadly and beautiful in the way that vipers are, lithe and ready to strike. I, with my long black hair, as dark as midnight and pale green eyes. They used to be darker, until my life was drained away from me.

My sisters were as equally fine. Lucia had tresses of cinnamon-brown hair and warm brown eyes that had seduced many a man. Victoria had pale skin and thick, red hair with golden threads to it. Together we looked to this man like three seraphs painted on a church ceiling; little did he know we were demons. He felt it though, in the deep recesses of his mind. I could smell his fear, a heady mixture along with his sweet scent of English heather and toffee. From across the room, I could hear his heartbeat increase in speed, from both terror and yearning.

As he looked at us, his desire rose and his manhood with it through the sheets. He seemed embarrassed, but that only inflamed me more. The blood that I had stolen coursed through me, and my nipples tightened in the anticipation of our union. I loved this power over him; I could probably send him to his climax with a single whisper, but then where would be the fun in that? All I had to do was cast a single glance in his direction; I would have this human begging at my feet.

It had been so long since anyone had loved me properly. The Count had withdrawn so much in the past few months that he barely gave us a passing glance. My own breath hitched as I looked at the sweet, delirious Jonathan Harker. My only desire greater than taking him into bed was taking him into death.

We gathered in a huddle at the edge of the door, moonlight streaming through the windows and illuminating our sharp smiles and sharper teeth. We were all eager.

I turned to the youngest of us. "You may go first," I said. "I know you are young and impatient." As if being older did anything for patience.

She shook her head, red, gentle curls bouncing. "You go. You are the eldest and yours is the right to go first," she said, and my other sister nodded in agreement.

The middle child turned to each of us and said, "And what of Victor? What if he finds out? He forbade us to touch this man."

That was Lucia. She was a true middle-born, always quick to caution, never wanting to tilt any side into anger or conflict.

I did. He would notice me, damnation, because he had spent far too long ignoring me. I did not care if he caught me, and if I incited his wrath, all the better, because it would give some indication that he still noticed me.

Slowly then, I turned, and walked languorously to the bed. My blood urged me to go faster, but I wanted to relish each moment, as I did not know when I would have another chance. As I stood over him, I leisurely took off my dress, more as a show for him than me. My nipples stood out in the cold, night air. If I seduced him as I truly wanted to, I would simply lift my hem, straddle him, and ride him until his heart gave out. But for that night, I wanted him as stiff as I could make him.

His heart beat faster, and mine picked up with it, as my hunter's instinct took over. Our hearts beat as one, hunter and prey, and I loved the anticipation of the kill. I drew back the covers, revealing his long, delightful member. I had had no idea that the English were so well endowed, and I licked my lips in anticipation. Straddling him, I bent my head to whisper to him.

"You are mine, and I shall have you tonight in all ways imaginable," I said. He shivered at my touch against the velvet softness of his ear, and goose flesh arose on his arms. Feeling his member pulse against my thigh, I began to kiss him on the forehead, then lower on his lips. His locked with mine, and I know he felt some brief guilt over the woman he had left in England.

Not too much guilt, apparently. He kissed me harder, and I drew my hands down his arms, locking them in an iron grip onto the bed. He fought against me for a moment, trying to lift his arms, feeling my inhuman strength, but I simply opened my mouth to let him in deeper inside me. His struggle, quaint as it was, stopped when he felt our tongues collide in a striking, twisted dance.

I broke away and began kissing his neck. He moaned, a deep, animal sound that made my sent my blood rushing and singing through my veins. My fangs withdrew, evidence of my craving, hard and sharp like needles, and I pressed them against his neck. I did not enter him just yet, but simply letting him know what would inevitably happen.

My kisses roamed farther down his throat, to his collarbones, his chest, and waist. His member was so stiff that it throbbed slightly, and I took it in my hand. I began to kiss it and this doomed man arched his back with need. My sisters watched, at times touching themselves, at times simply gazing on us, waiting until it was their turn. Taking him in my mouth, I sucked like I would soon suck his hot, rich blood.

Yes, now he was ready, and so was I.

Mounting him, I reveled in his expression of utter submission and pleasure. I rocked my hips forward, riding his body, feeling each pulse as our heartbeats merged together. His pleasure grew, and I felt his member grow stiff with the need to release, but I would not let him. This man was mine until I deemed otherwise.

The feelings grew more intense, and I rode him until I was ready to let go and fall into that tiny death, that shuddering bliss.

At that instant, Victor burst through the door.

He grabbed me by the hair and yanked me off Jonathan. I winced in pain and fell back. He flung me to my sisters, and they helped steady me from the force of his throw.

"I told you that you were not to touch him!" he yelled. His face was distorted with rage and at that moment, I feared for my life, immortal though it was. "I have forbidden it while he is here."

Colliding with my sisters, they looked guilty and threw me dirty looks. I saw [Name] mouth the words, *I told you*, and I would be sure to pinch her later until a bruise formed.

"You cannot forbid us from having our fun and nourishing ourselves at the same time," I replied. "You have never cared before."

"[Name], you have always been strong-willed, but you go too far, this time!" he said. My sisters flinched as his words rang out.

What of it?" I yelled to him. "Why is he so different? He is but a simple human after all."

"This man is mine," he said simply, his face still white with anger.

I pulled on my dress, nearly tearing it in my own heightened will. Jonathan lay deathly still on the bed, as if by pretending to be asleep or hypnotized would absolve him from Victor's wrath.

"What makes him so important?" I said. "You have thousands of humans at your disposal. You have never cared before if we lie with another man in your castle."

Victor paused, his chest heaving, his eyes blazing with hellish ire. "He is part of my plan," he said. "And I need him for a purpose. You will have him to yourself when that purpose is complete. But for now, Do. Not. Touch. Him," he said.

I walked up close to Victor, so close that our noses almost touched. My body was still pulsing from the interrupted dance between Jonathan and I, and I was still heated and inflamed.

"You leave us, then expect us to bow to you?" I said. "You have not loved us in so long. And yet you are angry that we would delight in another? You do not know how to love," I said.

My sisters glanced at each other at the vehemence of my words.

Gripping my arm, Victor took us out of the room. He threw me against the stone wall. A torchlight made the shadows flicker across his face.

"I do not fear you," I lied.

Victor kissed me deeply. I pressed myself against him and wrapped my legs around his. "I do know how to love," he said, his voice low. "And I will show you the power of my affection when I am through. But I will not allow you to touch him."

"Are you jealous?" I asked, hoping that he was.

"Of course not," he said. "But he must be kept alive. And you tend to get carried away with humans," he said, grinning wickedly.

"Just tell me why you need him," I begged, hating the sound of my own voice, how I needed to know his plans.

"I will not," he said. And he strode down the spiraling stairs and into the shadows.

Chapter 2

When I saw Berenice reading in the study room, her pale, creamy face framed by her dark, copper hair, my breath quickened. The fire crackled in the heart beside her, and she looked to be in deep, vampiric concentration. Beeswax candles stood in candelabra all around her, their burning filling the air with the aroma of honey. Although we did not eat as mortals did, we still enjoyed the same smells; it harkened back to the days when we could eat, and were tied to very powerful memories. In that moment, I remembered licking honey from a mortal boy's fingers, and I wanted to do the same to Berenice.

What took mortals weeks to read only took our vampire eyes and minds mere hours. Over the centuries, we had devoured Socrates, Descartes, and now the new lovers of knowledge, such as the German Heidegger, among others. My eyes glanced to the cover of the book.

Treasure Island, it read.

I saw her shift and take a breath, her lovely breast rising over her dress. The sight of her reading unraveled me, and I felt a powerful stirring grip me.

"Is it good?" I asked, walking over and bending over her chair. I feigned to look at the book, but it simply gave me a better view of the delightful V of her bosom.

"Exceptional," she replied, never taking her eyes from the page. They zoomed back and forth, as they scanned the words in front of her. "It speaks of pirates traversing the ocean," she said. "I wonder what it would be like to see it." She now sounded far away, becoming lost in the story again.

What indeed, would it be like to witness the ocean? I had read that it was grander than the mind could imagine.

Perhaps a mortal mind, I scoffed. Not mine.

Still, I hungered for the knowledge, and not for the first time, the bindings that kept me tied to the land chaffed me. Victor had said many times that if I ever left, I would die. My vampiric body was tied in some ineffable, mysterious way to the land, and once I crossed it, I would meet my final death.

I loved Berenice's mind; she was so much more serious than Claudia. Claudia was flighty, naughty, and saucy, but Berenice was always chasing after the deeper questions, questions that even I, with my five centuries, could not answer. Sometimes, she infuriated me with her questions, but that made me love her more.

Bending my head to her throat, I kissed her gently.

Let me steal your attention, I thought. Just for a moment.

Berenice closed her eyes. Her skin was soft, like the petals of a rose. I gently dabbed kisses to her cheeks, her forehead. I walked around the chair, so I could face her. Kissing her on the lips, she stole my breath when she opened her mouth for me.

Reaching my hand up, I grasped her luscious curve and began to softly stroke. I could feel the same fire in me that I knew was rising in her. With each caress, it felt as though I were pleasuring myself, giving pleasure to her. I ran my thumb over her puckered nipple, and she gasped.

That made my fangs distend.

I squeezed through the satin, while trailing my fingers up her thigh. The book fell to the floor, unnoticed. When my fingers found the bundle of nerves at the apex of her thighs, she moaned softly, like the coo of a dove.

She began kissing me back, fiercely. It was only when I heard another, more masculine groan that I turned around.

Victor was in the doorway, watching us. His eyes seemed lit up by the fire in the hearth. He watched us hungrily, greedily.

"Don't stop," he growled, low and commanding. "Keep going."

I grinned, slowly, and carefully raised Berenice's hem. "Do you mean like this—" My fingers continued to dance across Berenice, whose legs now shook. She would not be able to help herself; her pleasure was quickly reaching its ascent. "Or like this?" I slipped two fingers inside her and felt her shudder. I nearly reached my own devious heights watching her writhe and give into my touch and she rubbed herself against me.

Berenice was so sensitive.

In a flash, Victor was behind me. He grabbed my wrist.

"With me. Now," he said, his voice raspy with desire.

He pulled me out of the study, leaving Berenice to wallow in the afterglow of my affection.

Victor's grip on my wrist was like iron. As we moved through the labyrinth of corridors, I was proud that I had him so focused on me, so delirious with desire. When we reached the bedroom, he turned and pushed me onto the bed, so that I fell on my back into a cloud of softness.

"You do not care for this dress, do you not?" he asked.

He did not wait for my answer.

With one immense tug, he pulled my dress apart, ripping the bodice down the middle. My breasts spilled out, craving his touch. I loved the feel of my nakedness, my undisguised body before Victor's magnetic gaze. His expert mouth bent to my own nipple, and I was lost in a storm of sensation.

I needed him. I needed him inside me that very second.

My own vampiric hands reached up to his pants and undid the strings that bound them together. I took his thick, proud staff in my hand and guided it to my center.

"You're already ready," he growled, deep in his throat. "You enjoyed Berenice, I take it?"

He paused, hovering over me.

"Not nearly as much as you watching," I responded.

With that comment, Victor drove into me. He touched my core, the very space where my soul once used to reside. He pressed that deep, carnal part of me that would never tire of his touch. Filled with liquid fire, my hips arched to meet his. We rocked together in a frenzy, as wave after wave of sensation rolled through me, destroying me.

It was the sight of Victor's fangs that undid me. We knew exactly who the other was, all of our horrible, terrorizing ways, our self-destruction, our lust, our shared damnation. Where once I had feared those fangs, I now idolized them.

When I reached my peak, I cried out, Victor's name on my lips. He came soon after me, driving me further and further past the point of all consciousness, of any coherent thought.

Victor collapsed on top of me, and I relished his weight, his dark musk, his utterly powerful, feline grace.

Then, just as suddenly, he lifted his head and kissed me on the forehead.

"Meet me on the roof in five minutes," he said. He darted off me and began reassembling his clothes. "I have something important to tell you."

I was still swimming in the glow of him, in the only light that I would ever feel in my life again. If I had been cleverer, I would have been able to detect the note in his voice. I would have been terrified. As it was, the only thing I could feel was a warm, deep contentment.

"I need to hunt," I said. Now that my senses were slowly returning, I realized that I was ravenous.

"Fine," he said. "Be quick about it."
Always my master, always commanding.
He left the room, and I lay there, silently, on the bed.
I had no idea that what he would tell me would destroy my world.

Chapter 3

Scanning the cloudless sky, I knew that I would have to be quieter than usual if I wanted to make a kill. The moon was bright, and that meant that the humans, terrible though there eyesight was, would still be able to see some things, like a shadow darting past. No matter. It gave me an extra thrill, knowing that the difficulty was greater. After five hundred years of roaming the same land, I had come to know every inch, and it almost felt unfair at times to be able to so easily navigate. The poor humans were still blustering around, while I was queen of my own empire.

I slipped out of the castle, feeling my powerful legs under me, the buzz from Victor's passionate embrace, and the ravenous, unrelenting hunger that stayed with me. The closer I crept toward the humans, the more my throat hurt, feeling as though I were swallowing rocks or sand. Fiery, burning sand.

It was a need as deep as the one Victor gave me. I loved it. It tugged deep within, urging me onward. I was filled with renewed energy, and I practically flew over the earth toward the unsuspecting humans.

The wind shifted, and I smelled fire. My body instinctively tensed, but it was only the fire of late cooking, hearth fire, tucked deeply in the cottages. I could hear the sighs of the humans, even their heartbeats, from miles away. I could hear their beds creaking as they turned in them, tossing from uneasy sleep, as they knew, even in their dreams, that I was coming.

A twig snapped. I darted into the shadows.

Why was some poor, foolish human wandering around in the forest, alone, at night? Had he not heard the stories? Didn't he fear the monsters who preyed on his kind?

He soon would.

Creeping ever closer, I listened, as I heard the man's heartbeat increase. His sweat was pungent, drifting on the breeze. I raised my face and sniffed, pinpointing him. His footsteps were crooked; he had a limp. Excellent. Although I always loved a challenge, I was eager to return to Victor, to discover what he had to tell me.

Fool that I was.

It did not matter why this man was alone. It did not matter that he had a family waiting for him, that he would leave the earth and them to suffer without him.

His heartbeat was now wild. He knew I was close. I watched him from the shadows, making each step as light as a mountain panther.

The hackles on his neck stood up. He wiped a bead of sweat from his forehead.

He knew.

Oh, how he knew.

I pounced.

He did not even have time to cry out as I sunk my fangs into him.

After my ravishment with Victor, his hot, rich blood felt like ecstasy. Victor gave me a thirst that nothing could quench, except this. He took me to heaven, this man and his smooth, salty blood. Drinking deeply, I relished the feeling of his life force, this hellishly good liquid trailing down my throat.

It reminded me of Victor.

The pitiful human pounded weakly against me, but I caught his hand and clamped it to the ground, on which we were now sprawled.

"Please," he begged. "My family…"

I briefly lifted my head, releasing him. His head lolled to the side, as he had already lost strength in his limbs.

I shrugged. I proceeded to drink some more.

What did I care for this human and his family? This human existed for no other purpose than to give me life, to sustain me. He was no better than the cows or sheep he ate. His blood now filled my veins, gave me the appearance of life. Color flooded my cheeks, and I felt my body absorbing the dark ichor like a flower in need of rain.

I heard a thudding in my head. His heart. Soon it would stop. I loved this part, this ultimate release. The vibration trembled through me, and I shuddered with the magnificent pleasure of it. If loving Victor was half this good, I would never leave the bed again. No matter what became of Victor (a blasphemous thought, I know), I would always, always need this. This touched my very soul, vibrated through my mind, my entire being.

Colors danced before my eyes. The man gasped; his soul left him in a great, resounding shudder.

I cannot describe to you what it felt like to take his soul, to feel it leave his body. The ecstasy of the blood and the rich, hot, release of his death. It was so much greater than sex, so much purer, holier, refined by eons of vampiric need.

I dropped his body, watched it slump to the ground. Delicately, I wiped my mouth. Victor always said that I was a messy eater, and that it shamed him to see blood around my mouth, but if one could not have fun with one's sustenance, what was the damn point?

Leaving him for the sun and the crows to find, I sped away into the night, to my lover and my destruction.

Chapter 4

"You're leaving?"

My heart, if it had still the impulse to beat, would have leapt to my throat. As it was, all I could do was stand there, open-mouthed, feeling a weight constrict in my chest.

We were standing on the roof of the castle. My sisters were slated from our nightly amusements, and Victor had brought me up here to tell me that he had news. A new villagers was news; a silly, arrogant priest who had been caught dangling another young maiden on his knee was news. This was torture; this was an earthquake.

"Yes," he replied swiftly, turning his face to the shimmering moonlight. The moon was bright and full, a pearl against black velvet. It was so bright that I could see the crags and mountains on its surface, mirroring our own dark, rugged land. "Mr. Harker has been helping me establish my plans for England. That is why you are under the strictest of orders not to touch him."

I could feel the order binding me. It was as potent as a rope. He was my maker, and I could not disobey. Not even if I wanted to.

"England," I repeated dully. England, what did I know of that pitiful country that dared take my beloved away from me? The borders of lands had changed so often in the past centuries that I often forgot which was which nowadays. Human borders were for humans; I had mine, around the land of my family, my people. I could not cross it, unless I wanted to die.

"Yes, England," he said. "You know, that little island that lies on the coast of the great Atlantic Ocean."

My mind whirled to a map. Ah yes. Land of rain and gray, drizzly clouds. Victor had told us of it many times.

"Why do you want to go *there*?" I asked. Why indeed, would he want to leave the land of beautiful, rugged mountains, of shadows and dark pines, and an endless supply of blood? My cloak whipped around me in the wind, and I held my gravity perfectly. A human would have been too afraid at this height of falling.

Victor smiled his cat-like grin. "Because it is quickly becoming the center of the world," he said. "That American continent is up-and-coming, I will say, but England has been on the rise for the past two centuries, and I doubt that they will stop now."

Victor leaped to a nearby spire, grasping it with one hand, his preternatural strength a wonder for anyone to behold. He swept his arm around, gesturing toward the horizon. "Power, Amelia. We have been too indolent these past few centuries. It is time to come out of our modest means of living and enter into the affairs of men on a grand scale. England is the key to power, and I will have it."

I leapt to the spire with him, leaning in close. "You do not have to go anywhere to seek power," I said. "You are the ruler of this kingdom here."

"A tiny kingdom. A beggar's kingdom."

If I had a heart, it would have been hurt. Rubbing my chest to ease the insult away, I tried a different tact.

"But we will be so lonely here," I said, pouting my lips, giving him my best playfully-sad face. I hope that he could not see that I was not playing. "Who will love us and keep us warm when the winter snows come?"

"You are more than capable of keeping each other warm," he said, kissing me briefly on the lips. "As I have witnessed many times." He leapt from the spire back onto the roof.

I gave a huff of indignation.

"Why now?" I asked. "When will you leave?"

"Tomorrow," he replied. "Immediately after moonrise."

Tomorrow!

I nearly choked. I felt a powerful, dizzying rush that I had not felt in so long. It was cold, brittle, and made me feel thus. Fear. He was leaving, and I did not know how to live without him.

He had not left my side in centuries, and now he wanted to go galivanting off to some foreign, hell-forsaken place to trot around with blue bloods, mingling with popes and kings?

Jumping from the spire, reveling in my own strength, I landed beside him with no more sound than the touch of lips on silk.

I pressed my chest into him. "Surely there is no need to rush," I said, stroking his chest with my hand. My hand continued its southward path. "You've waited this long; surely you can wait a little longer." I was stroking something that, indeed, was becoming longer. "And longer…"

Victor closed his eyes. I loved giving him this pleasure as much as I did receiving it. "And longer…" I whispered into his ear.

He was now bulging, straining against his pants.

I smiled. He would stay.

Suddenly, he seized my hand.

He moved, so fast that even I could not see him, twisting my arm behind my back, trapping me. He stood behind me, and I could feel his bulge pushing into my ample backside. Pressing his nose against my hair, he inhaled and chuckled. "You are my favorite, I hope you know, Amelia," he said. "You always were. And you always will be."

He tightened his grip on me, and I felt that familiar, undiminished pulse of pleasure rush through me.

"However, it is quite time that we grow this little family of ours."

My heart, if I had one, if it were not already still, would have stopped. I knew what he meant, although I pretended to be a fool, to drag this moment out, to try to delay the inevitable.

"What?" I said, my body tensing against his statement. I could not believe it. Surely my ears had not heard the words that he just said?

Surely I must be going crazy or that I had not drank sufficient blood for the night.

He released me, turning me around to face him.

"Ah Amelia, you three are what I've known for so long," he said. "It is time. Don't you want another companion? There are so many delicious possibilities out there for us."

No.

I did not want another companion. I felt the flush of an emotion that I had not felt in nearly five centuries. It was hot, thorny, and ugly: jealousy. He could take as many women, or men, as he wanted, and I would not bat an eyelash. He could take any of my sisters, so long in the blood now that I had learned to love each of them like my own soul. But to make another vampire? Never!

I pushed him away. "And you are the only one I've known," I said. "And I do not need another! You are all I want. You are all I need."

Why could I not be enough for him? Why could he not simply stay here forever, our carnal nights flowing into each other in one long, unending dream? Victor had become my world, and he was ripping that away.

Victor walked to the edge of the castle rooftop. Already he was putting distance between myself and him, and it was killing me.

"Soon, you'll see," he whispered. "I have so many plans for us."

"Victor, please," I said, striding over to him, throwing myself at his feet. I gripped his legs, kissed his feet. "I will do anything that you ask, but please, do not go. Do not leave me alone."

"Get up. Do not debase yourself thus," he said. His voice had turned as harsh as gravel, and I was humiliated with myself, but I could not let go. I would not let go.

"Please," I whispered. My grip tightened.

"Enough!"

The command cracked over my head, the strength of the magic urging me to release my maker, but I could not.

Victor took a step away from the edge, and I launched up, knocking him to the ground. I fell on him, placing my entire weight against his frame. My hands locked around his wrists, and I tried to restrain him, tried to bind my beautiful, evil, enchanting Victor.

He whipped his wrists quickly, and in one motion, threw me off. I should have known better than to try to restrain him, but I could not help it. He grabbed me, and launched me against the wall, my head slamming back against the rough stone. Victor's eyes locked with mine, and I saw anger, bright, savage anger, and worst of all: disappointment. I had disappointed my Victor, and that hurt worst of all.

He pressed his fangs to my throat, and I welcomed the bite, prayed that it would come. It would hurt, and it would heal, and it would keep us together, for one more moment at least.

But he did not bite. His teeth did not break my skin.

He gave a short, quick laugh.

"You will always be my favorite," he said. "And I will have to punish you for your insolence." I felt the sharp, hard teeth against my cold skin, and I willed this moment to last.

"Yes, do it," I whispered, closing my eyes. "Punish me."

"When I return," he whispered in reply, and at once, I felt his hands leave me.

When I opened my eyes, I was alone.

Victor had gone.

Chapter 5

I couldn't stand it. Victor was gone, and he had left a gaping hole in my chest.

Of course, he had left before. He would hunt and feed someplace, else, going deep into the mountains, or prowl the other, wilder places of the world, where he was free to roam. Unlike us. He always that that he had the ability to leave, because he was the original vampire, and thus, he had more power than his offspring. That made sense. So he could leave, and we had to stay behind.

But never like this.

I knew that when he left this time, it was different. I knew that when he talked of "expanding the family," he meant to create an army of vampires. Not just one or two like he had with my sisters through the hundreds of years that we had known each other. We were as tightly bound as the threads in a rope, and Victor wanted to break that. I loved my sisters like my own soul, if I had one. We were a family, didn't he understand that? We were a clan, and we had no need of another! He wanted to diminish the bond by creating more, *more*. Where had that pitiful dissatisfaction come from? Where had the desire to propagate more vampires suddenly sprung?

I curled my lip in disgust. I was pacing back and forth in the castle walls, my bare feet tapping on the stone floor. I barely felt the cold. It only registered as a sensation to my vampire body, not pain. I hardly ever felt pain.

Except now.

Staring at a tapestry on the wall, I took note of its brilliant colors, the happy, forest scene where maidens frolicked with animals and minstrels sang in the background. I ripped it down and tore it in two with my bare hands.

"Victor!" I screamed, although I knew that he could not hear me, not even with his supernatural heaing. He was too far away by now, on his course to that cursed land called England. I flung the tapestry away from me.

Power, he had said. Bah! Didn't we already have power enough? We were rulers of the night, king and queens of darkness. The villagers feared us, made up stories about us, and we had become living legends. We were immortal, free from the threat of disease or old age. We could only die by fire, the sun, and crossing from our homeland. At least, we offspring would die; Victor as the eldest would survive even that.

I swung my arms and pushed everything from the table before me. Candles and books scattered onto the floor, papers falling down as gentle as snow.

My dress swished around my ankles as I walked up and down the hallway. I was boiling with rage and fear. Yes, fear, fear that things were changing.

I glanced up. My feet had led me to the bedroom. When my eyes fell on the bed, I took two strides toward it, faster than any mortal eye could follow, and began to rip at the sheets and pillows. I tore them, and feathers burst from the seams, floating around me. I demolished the four wooden posters, splintering them with my bare hands.

In my hundreds of years as a vampire, nothing had changed. Everything had remained the same among us. When my sisters were born into the blood, I had welcomed them as humans might welcome kittens into a new home. I had not minded their arrival into my life, because Victor had said that I needed companionship, and in my early years, when I was two hundred, I agreed with him. One, yes. Even two sisters I tolerated.

But more?

No. I could not tolerate this.

Suddenly, I felt very, very tired.

I slumped against the flor, the remaining feathers drifting around me. Glancing out the window, I suddenly felt the weight of my five hundred years. Yes, we were immortal, but sometimes I thought that our souls were still human, as illogical as that seemed, and that they were not meant to last longer than one-hundred twenty.

Tears rolled down my cheeks, fresh, hot blood-tears. I could not cry any other way.

The moon seemed to beckon me from the window, curling a bony-white finger toward me. It seemed to say, "If you cannot live without Victor, can you live at all?"

I stood. I knew what I would do. If Victor did not want to live with me, then I would save him that heartache. I would not live, then.

Rising to my feet, I left the castle. I did not say goodbye to my sisters. As my feet touched the silky, obsidian grass, it felt as though they knew where to carry me.

They will not miss me, I thought, my own twisted thoughts becoming twisted lies in my mind. *They are still young. They will love whoever else Victor brings.*

How much pain was I in, to not see that they would miss me so! I could not see it; I could not see anything beyond my rage and my helplessness. I could not go on without Victor. It was as though he were leaving me behind, and of course, he already had.

My legs raced over the land, my feet only just barely touching the ground before springing back up again. Trees and rocks darted past me in a blur. Animals were too slow to respond to my presence, only moving until after I had already passed. I was the Angel of Death in a ruby dress.

I reached the border between my homeland and the outside world. I knew it was here from the way the mountains crossed before me, the valley spread out below. I had never crossed the valley before; Victor had warned me so many times not to do it. He swore that I would die once I crossed that threshold, the point of no return. Yet here I was, staring into my own fate like a witch staring into her cauldron. What would it be like to die, I wondered. And how would it happen? Would I simply seize up, never to move again? Crumble to dust? Burst into flames?

I did not know, and the response would not change my course of action, not even a sliver. As I stood staring at my beautiful country before me, I gave a small moment of grace to it. Bending to touch my lips to the earth, I gave thanks for all that it had given me, for all that had allowed me to live this far. Five hundred years was enough, I tried to convince myself. Five hundred years was plenty. I had had a family; it simply had not been enough for my king, my owner, my savior.

Taking a deep breath, I walked into the valley. My knees did not shake, and my breath did not quicken. I held my head high. I thought that I heard my heart echo in my ears, but it must have been a trick of the wind; my heart had not beat for five hundred years.

I walked out of the valley. The air was no different here. The sky was still the same, lit up with a thousand diamond-stars, blazing down on me, caressing me with their heavenly light. I kept walking. I expected any moment to meet the final black, to be consumed by a power, to be released from my body forever.

Nothing happened.

Frowning, I kept walking, deeper into the woods that hemmed in the valley. These woods were completely and utterly foreign to me. In five hundred years, I had come to know every single inch of my forest, every rock, every creature, every shifting, growing tree. This place was completely foreign to me, and I loved it. I loved how the new earth smelled, how different flowers bloomed in this part of the forest, how different creatures scurried by. Astounding!

The newness was almost overwhelming. How long would I enjoy the forbidden pleasure of a new land? I had set my feet in a place where they had never been before, and I shivered in delight. I stopped walking and looked around. I was still alive. That is, I had not met the final death.

Enlightenment began to bloom in my mind. It was as though a plant was impossibly growing from stone, as I sometimes saw in the castle. I reached my hands up and clutched my head, the new knowledge cracking me, undoing me.

I had not died.

That meant Victor had lied.

I fell to my knees. Emotions flitted through me in rapid succession. Disbelief, amazement, utter astonishment gave way to quiet, unbridled wrath.

For five hundred years, I had been confined to a castle in a small country. I had never been able to leave, to see the world, to watch it change and melt and mold into something different.

He had confined me, kept me prisoner. Only now was I realizing just how deep my prison had extended. I had had the ability to leave all this time, and never once had he let me. He had held me captive not only in the physical land, but in my own mind as well.

I felt my shackles shift into something different.

Oh, I was still beholden to him. Still I felt the deep connection between us, but now it was something far more sinister. I would never let it go.

I looked, far beyond the mountains, far past the twisting shadows into a realm that I had never dared to touch.

I would go to England, track Victor down, and kill him.

Chapter 6

When Miss Lucy Westenra opened the door to her lovely London townhome, Quincy Morris knew immediately that she would reject him.

He gripped the enormous bouquet of flowers in his hands too tightly, the thorns from the roses digging into his skin. He thought that Lucy had never looked more lovely than she did in her sky blue dress. It accentuated her startlingly blue eyes and made the pale golden of her hair seem even softer, more delicate, just like Lucy herself. Lucy opened the door with a huge smile on her face, but Quincy's faltered, for he saw in her eyes that her mind was already made up, and nothing that he said would change it.

"Gracious heavens, Quincy, you shouldn't have!" Lucy said, when she saw the forest of roses, sprigs of lavender, and delicate marigolds he held. Taking them immediately in a tiny, graceful hand, she inhaled deeply and closed her eyes.

How very much like an angel she looks, he thought. It made the inevitability of her rejection that much more poignant. He loved her, and if it was her happiness that she wanted, then he would let her go for that.

"Good after—" Quincy began, but something caught in his throat. He cleared it and started again. "Good afternoon, Miss Westenra."

Lucy was the perfect London Society girl—wealthy, bubbly, eager to talk about the latest gossip, none too keen on politics or heavier subjects. Perhaps Quincy would have preferred that she knew at least a little about the wider world around her, but then again, she looked so lovely when she tilted her head and her curls fell in a cloud around her face. Her laughter set at ease any preoccupation that she did not care to talk about poetry or art and instead desired to visit the Opera only to compare jewels with some countess or other.

Lucy looked over the tops of the flowers, her delicate eyelashes like butterfly wings. "Oh Quincy, you cad, you know you can call me Lucy." She turned to the interior of the house and called, "Father, Quincy is here."

A portly man in a brown vest and monocle came waddling down the hall. "Quincy, old boy!" He said, shaking Quincy's hand in a damp handshake. "How's those knives of yours coming along?"

Quincy tilted his head. "Getting better every day, sir." Quincy was part of an exclusive club that taught its members how to throw and fight with knives. It claimed that it was a more elegant way of fighting than with pistols, but in truth, Quincy simply enjoyed the skill it took to bury metal in a target some twenty feet away.

Lucy made a face. "I don't know why you bother with those silly knives," she said. "Seems awfully barbaric to me."

Mr. Westenra turned to Quincy and winked. "Ah women. They never understand the pleasures of hunting, eh?" Ushering Quincy inside, Mr. Westenra said, "So what brings you to my humble home, Quince?"

Quincy winced. He had never liked that nickname. "Well, I would like to ask your daughter something, sir." Mr. Westenra of course, knew this already. Quincy had asked him the day before and Lucy's father had given his consent.

"Of course," he replied. "Speaking of knives, I do believe I need to tell the scullery maid to sharpen the kitchenware. I could barely slice through the butter last night." Mr. Westenra gave a final wink and waddled away.

It was all part of the show and dance surrounding courtship of London. Sometimes, Quincy wished that he could simply speak what was on his mind right then, take Lucy, or any woman, for that matter, into his arms and whisk her away, without the pageantry. Of course, Quincy understood why these tacit rules where in place—after all, they weren't savages—but for once, Quincy simply wanted to give into his baser impulses.

It would have saved him the painful humiliation of going through the charade. Now he still had to ask, and she still had to give her answer.

As they sat down on separate couches, Quincy admired the paintings that adorned the walls, the tasteful, gilded ceilings, and marble fireplace. It looked a tad too feminine for someone of Mr. Westenra's position and disposition, as though a woman with loads of expendable income could afford to redecorate however she pleased—which of course, Lucy could and did.

Fresh flowers adorned every possible surface, but the bouquets looked as though they were meant to woo Lucy, not charm her with pastoral sweetness.

Quincy's stomach clenched. Someone else had been here before him. He briefly wondered whether his timing would have made a difference. Would she have said yes to him, if he had come a day sooner? An hour?

A clock ticked in the distance, and it grated on Quincy. Each second seemed to stretch out.

"Well, Miss W—" he began.

Lucy tilted her head and gave him a coy smile.

"Lucy," he corrected. "I came to ask you..."

Please marry me, he thought. Please be my companion and wife. Please allow me the wonderful pleasure of looking at those heavenly eyes every day.

"If you would accept my proposal to be my wife," he finished.

Lucy smiled, and Quincy felt as though one of his knives had entered his heart. He would indeed know what that exact sensation felt like in a matter of weeks, as his own knife plunged into his chest. But for now, he merely smiled back, as though he were not secretly dying inside.

"My darling Quincy," she began.

How he loved to hear his name upon her sweet, sensual mouth!

"I love you, you know," she said, not realizing the impact her words had on him. "We have been friends for ever so long, have we not?"

Quincy nodded; it was the only thing he could do.

"And you know that I adore your company," she continued, oblivious to the pain she was putting him through. "But I must say that although you have many charms that any woman would give any woman satisfaction—"

Any woman except you, he thought.

"I must decline your wonderful offer," she finished.

Quincy said nothing, and the only sound was the incessant ticking of the damned clock. The silence hung heavy between them, and Quincy felt the hot flush of embarrassment creep up his neck.

"I see," he said evenly.

"Oh Quincy, do not turn from me so! Do not hate me," said Lucy, springing from her seat on the couch and coming to sit beside him. "Promise me that you do not hate me."

Quincy swallowed his sadness. He could not let the beautiful Lucy see how much she had hurt him.

"Of course I do not hate you, my dear," he said. "But if I may ask...why?"

Lucy glanced away, fingering the edge of couch.

"Dearest Quincy, that question is so unfair. Can you ask the sun why it shines or why the river flows to the ocean?" She shook her head but moved closer to him on the couch. Their legs touched, and it was all Quincy could do to concentrate on Lucy's words. "No, you cannot, so please, do not ask why my heart beats for another. All that you need to know is that although my heart already belongs to someone else, you will always be my friend." She pouted her full, lovely lips. "You will always be my friend, won't you Quincy?" she said, grasping his hand.

How could he say no? He loved Lucy, was held in her sway and wanted to always stay in her life, however he could.

"On my honor as a gentleman, I promise that we will always be friends," he said. He paused. "However, may I ask who it is that is so fortunate to have gained your admiration and love?"

He was not sure that he even wanted to know the answer, but something, pride perhaps, pricked at him, and drove him to know.

Lucy leaned forward, pressing her ample bosom against his chest, and Quincy sucked in his breath. She tilted her head toward his ear, and her lips pressed softly against it. As she whispered, a shiver of delight went through Quincy, and he felt his loins stirring.

"Arthur Holmwood," she whispered. "I admit, he is not as thrilling to look at as you, dearest Quincy, but..." Lucy's hand slid up to the side of his face. "Let us say that when he becomes Lord Holmwood and comes into his inheritance, his face will not be so pitiful to look upon."

Then her lips moved to his mouth.

Quincy was startled, then quickly succumbed to the kiss. He was even more surprised when Lucy opened her mouth and lazily intertwined her tongue with his, kissing him deeply, fully.

Lucy released him after a few moments, Quincy dizzy and half-delighted, half-brokenhearted.

"That was a farewell kiss," she said, rising to her feet. "I hope that you meet the love of your life soon, Quincy. You deserve a love of your own."

Quincy quickly rose too, adjusting himself so that she (nor her father) could see the bulge that had started to press against his pants.

"Thank you, Lucy, but I do not think that I will ever meet anyone quite like you," he said.

"Well, you are right about that," she said, as they approached the front door. "But you will meet someone soon, Quincy. I can feel it in my bones."

Quincy stood on the threshold.

"I wish I could say the same," he said.

He tipped his hat and strode away.

Chapter 7

The first thing that I had to do was steal a map. I knew enough from seeing Victor's maps scattered along his table that I would not be able to go very far if I did not know where I was going.

I had to keep my rage in check, for a few hours at least. I would have to break into the home of someone who looked wealthy enough to own a map; most of the peasants would be illiterate, let alone own something as valuable as a map. Therefore, I would have to track down someone in possession of the key to my escape, make them explain it to me (for Victor never bothered, even when I had begged him to show me how to read one), and escape. I could not very well kill the human I needed to steal from.

So, pushing all direct thoughts of Victor aside, I prowled the countryside. It did not take long to find an opulent mansion, equal to that of Victor's. I smashed a window intentionally to let myself in. Normally, if I wanted to hunt, I loved the quiet chase, the skulking and the creeping. However, upon this lovely, lovely night, I needed them to know that I was there.

Sure enough, footsteps came pattering through the halls.

"Who's there?" cried the deep, bass voice of a man trying to conceal his fear. He clutched a fire poker in his hand, the pathetic lout. I could easily disarm him.

Which I did.

With one hand clutched around his throat, I bared my fangs for him to see.

"Take me to your maps," I said. I squeezed his throat harder. "And no games, human."

The man nodded, and I released him. Trembling, he walked to a similar version of Victor's study, with books, a writing desk, and, behold, an assortment of maps. I ignored the stench of the man's fear; he had wet himself upon knowing that he dealt with a monster.

Clutching a handful of maps, I laid them all on the table. There was only one problem: they were enormous. They were bulky and cumbersome, and they would slow me down, even with my vampiric speed.

Turning swiftly to him, I said, "Smaller human, I need something smaller."

The human moved his lips, but I heard nothing.

"Speak up!"

"I said, do you want maps of the world or only this city?"

"The world."

The word on my tongue tasted as sweet as blood, as sweet as the memory of honey.

He lifted a trembling finger. "The desk," he said, his voice quivering.

In a flash, I was ripping the drawers out of the desk. Papers, quills, and ink scattered over the floor as I looked for what I sought.

At last!

I seized a parchment, soft from use. It held the details of the land between here and the city of London.

The man was trying to slowly sneak out the door. Out of the corner of my eye, I saw him, slowly trying to edge his way out of the study. I raced over to him, grabbed him by the collar, and threw him into the first chair I saw.

"Show me how to read it," I demanded.

The man made a sign of the cross over himself.

That won't help you, human, I thought.

But he did. It took several boring reassurances that I would not, in fact, kill him or his family.

"I already drank," I said, as if that explained everything.

It irked me somewhat that I had to rely on a human to navigate my way in the world, but there it was. Another thing for Victor to answer for. Another way in which he had crippled me.

As soon as the pitiful human had shown me how to locate myself upon the earth using the map, I was off.

Nothing could stop me now.

MY EYES MARVELED AT the changes the world had wrought in nearly six hundred years. Magnificent cathedrals and castles towered above me in Budapest, and the streets were paved. The poor lived in filthy conditions, made even dirtier by the bizarre machines I saw. Ships going up rivers, spewing smoke; enormous, iron snakes winding their way through the forests, also belching smoke. I hissed when I saw these and avoided them. They moved too fast for me to trust, huge, hulking monstrosities. They looked like segmented worms, with wheels. They, too, blew smoke into the air.

The world was a far busier place than I had left it. People moved more quickly, sure of themselves and of their place in their society. Cities were enormous; I had never seen so many people in one place before.

I dined on the Danube river, loving the luxury of Budapest, with its casual seediness, its decadent splendor. There were so many people, I did not need to worry about a shortage or going hungry.

Every night, I buried myself within a graveyard or some deep basement. However I had survived crossing out of my country, I could not be sure that I would survive the sun. During the day, I raced along the ground, mile after mile disappearing under my fleet feet. I would reach London in a matter of days. As I coursed through the land they now called the Austro-Hungarian Empire, my one burning thought was how I would kill my lover.

The pain spurred me on ever quicker. With each mile, each step, I thought of the many ways I would end Victor's life. My fantasies grew dark and twisted, yet the blood tears fell from my eyes every night. Sometimes in grief, sometimes in anger, but always in exquisite agony.

From Budapest, I wandered through Prague, its quaint spires rising up through the air. Then on to Frankfurt, the tongue of its native people drifting into a rougher version of its Germanic ancestor. With each passing city, my mind expanded and threatened to topple. There was so much to see, so much to explore, so many people to taste; I wanted it all. I wanted the cool, slippery light of the moon on my skin as I traveled down the Danube; I wanted to contemplate the stars on top of the magnificent cathedrals of this modern world; I wanted to inhale the sweet air of new mountains, new flowers.

My dreams tormented me at night. They were of smaller demons stabbing at me with iron fire pokers. They demanded to know why I had never left, why I had never seen any of these beautiful sites before.

I did not know what to tell them.

Finally, I moved into the city of Calais, becoming quite charmed by the French people. They drank so much wine that I tasted it in their blood; it gave notes of cedar and berries to my normal coppery drink, and I loved them all the more for it. They were so proud, the French, thinking that they ruled the world, when in fact my sisters and Victor did.

My destination was a mere Channel crossing now; I would soon be in the same city as Victor, and from there, he would be easily found.

Oh yes, I knew where Victor would go. Through the centuries, I had come to know him better than perhaps I knew myself. Victor was easily knowable, and that was what made him vulnerable and weak.

He loved beauty. To be specific, he loved feminine beauty. If he wanted to make a new vampire, or a host of new vampires, he would start with going to where there were the most beautiful females of all.

When I first saw the ocean, I wept. I had to conceal the blood tears as I stood on the deck of the pitching, rocking deck of the ship. I inhaled the sharp, tang of salty air, and felt the magnificent sea breeze blow my hair into tangles. The water extended into infinity, and I finally felt like I had something to describe my eternal isolation, the immensity of my eternity. The ocean knew; the ocean understood. The blue-black of the sea and sky melded together, and I thought of Victor and I. Once you saw far enough into the distance, the line between them disappeared. Victor and I had been together for so long that our distinctions shimmered and vanished into time.

On board, the captain had not minded when a beautiful woman with plenty of money (stolen on the way, of course, from the corpses I left behind) only wanted to peek out of her cabin at night. Even better if she did not eat much, for that meant more supplies to go around for the rest of the seafarers.

When I arrived on land, the first thing that I noticed was the hideous stench. The city smelled absolutely awful. Animal and human waste mixed together, along with burning pitch, garbage, and that awful smoke that kept spilling out of ships made of iron. I supposed that I would have to get used to it. At that moment, I had a pang of longing for my old home. The air was so clean and pure in the mountains, and I had never appreciated it before. This air felt like inhaling a miasma of fetid, rotting refuse.

As I stepped off the ship, I immediately spotted a woman who could help me. I knew this woman, for I had been her once. She had the look of one already-dead, her soul numbed, and her dignity shattered. Her face was painted, her clothes revealed skin to entice men to buy her body for a night.

I walked up to her. "Where can I find the best market of flesh?" I asked. If this woman was not connected to it directly, surely she would know someone who was.

"Piss off, then," she said. She glared at me.

How dare this woman speak to me thus! I would have grabbed her by the throat, but the throngs of people deterred me from doing so. I needed to blend into the crowd. In the vastness of my mountain village, I could creep in the shadows, but I had no experience with crowds.

Fortunately, I knew how to deal with people like her.

I proffered her a few gold coins, then motioned for her to speak.

Once she bit the coin, she shoved it deep into a pocket of her dress. "Breath of the Angels," she said. "Across from old Benny, then six streets up. Looks like a church but it ain't."

I nodded. But one thing still eluded me. "Who is Benny?" I asked.

The woman looked at me as though I were the idiotic one.

"Ben," she said. "Big Ben. You know, the huge bloomin' clock?" And she pointed out the tower for me.

Only nodded, I left the woman.

"Bloody foreigners," I heard the woman mumble.

Her insult did not matter to me. Killing her would only waste time on my hunt for Victor. Now that I knew where to go, I raced to murder the one who killed me.

Chapter 8

Quincy stared at the carriages going by, the clopping of the horses hooves on the cobblestones oddly comforting. He felt as though his heart were being trampled upon, and he was glad to know of a sound that described it. As he meandered up and down the streets of London, he found himself wandering into a public house. A pint might cheer him up. Or two. Or three. Queen Victoria might frown upon them, but they were all the rage now, with the houses a place for the classes to mingle and forget about their worries for a little while.

As he entered the door, the raucous conversation helped drown out any thoughts in his mind. Lucy symbolized everything to him: a good girl, proper upbringing, and a lovely face that might have graced his children. Alas, it was not to be.

When he ordered his beer, he heard a voice behind him.

"Quincy! What the devil are you doing here?"

He half-turned, as someone clapped him on the shoulder.

"Hello, Jonathan," he said. "Weren't you on some expedition to Transylvannia?"

Jonathan Harker turned a bit pale. "Yes," he said. "Thankfully, that is terminated." He then shut down, and Quincy could tell that Jonathan did not want to speak of it any longer. "So again, chap, what brings you hear?"

"Here you go, love," said the barmaid as she gave Quincy his pint. He eyed her ample breast as she flounced away.

Quincy took a long draught before answering. "A proposal gone sour," he replied.

Jonathan drank from his own full (but quickly disappearing) glass. "That's bum luck, mate. Who was the object of your affections?"

"Lucy Westenra."

Jonathan nearly spat out his beer from laughing. "Lucy Westenra! Good god, man, everyone knows that she's in love with Arthur Holmwood's estate," he said, shaking his head. "If it's love you're looking for, you may need to search a bit harder."

Quincy finished off his beer and ordered another. The pain was not yet gone, and he needed it to vanish. "I'm not sure what it is I'm looking for," he murmured.

Jonathan peered at Quincy. "You *are* in love with her, you poor bastard," he said. He leaned in closer to Quincy. "Listen, if you need a way to dull the pain in your heart, I know of a place. They have the best snatch that money can buy, it's a classy establishment, not like the filthy slum women you might see on the street."

Quincy raised an eyebrow at his friend and drank again. "Aren't you engaged to Mina?" he asked.

Jonathan grinned. "I am and happily so; that does not mean that I did not take a stroll down the garden of earthly delights once in a while," he said. Jonathan polished off his drink and set the cup down. "I've sworn it off now. In truth, I love Mina so much that she's the only one I need. I can't imagine myself going there now." He clapped Quincy on the shoulder again. "But to get over a grieving heart, it might be just the thing for you."

Quincy thought about it, the beer loosening his reserve. "Where is it?"

Jonathan scribbled down the address on a loose newspaper and handed it to Quincy. "They're called the Breath of the Angels, and you have to know the password. It's 'Heaven Sent.'"

Jonathan glanced at his pocket watch. "Speaking of my beloved, I'm to meet her in half an hour," he said, paying for his and Quincy's drinks. "Go on. Enjoy. Forget about Lucy."

Quincy paused. "How did you know that you loved Mina? How did you find her?"

As he put on his coat, Jonathan thought. "Honestly, she found me. And as for loving her? That's easy." He put on his hat. "I knew that I loved her when I knew that I would die for her."

Jonathan left the public house.

Quincy gripped the slip of newspaper in his hand. It was absurd. It was foolish. No decent gentleman in London would dare go to such an establishment.

And of course, he went.

Chapter 9

As Jonathan Harker left the public house, he felt a pang of sympathy for his friend Quincy. The poor sop, he had looked absolutely destroyed. What did men see in Lucy Westenra anyway? She was simply a tedious, London Society girl, who could not think even if two thoughts collided in her head.

Still, Mina, the love of his life, was friends with her, for whatever reason. If Lucy had just finished giving old Quincy the boot, she must have had her sights set on Arthur.

At the corner of the street, Jonathan decided to go to Lucy's house, to check up on her. Mina was always saying that he needed to take an interest in her friends more; well, now he was doing it. He glanced at his pocket watch again and surveyed the setting sun. It would be dark soon, but he would have time before he met up with Mina.

He ran the bell and Lucy answered.

"Jonathan, dear!" she exclaimed.

How shrill her voice sounds, he thought.

"Hello Lucy," he replied. "Heard you threw our boy Quincy into the street."

Lucy pouted; Jonathan admitted, she was quite good at doing that. "Do not hate me, Jonathan. I simply am not in love with him."

Jonathan put his hands into his pockets. "So it's to be Arthur, then is it?"

Lucy nodded. "He really seems to be the perfect match for me."

Him or his money? Jonathan thought but refrained from saying anything.

"Well, I simply wanted to stop by and check on you. Mina sends her regards and thanks you for the absolutely splendid engagement gift."

Lucy waved a hand in the air. "Think nothing of it. I only want the best for my dear Mina, and you, Jonathan, are it." Lucy paused. "Jonathan, are you all right? You've gone quite pale."

Jonathan's gaze was fixed on the figure approaching from the end of the sidewalk.

No, he thought. *It can't be. It can't be him.*

His heart started racing. Before his eyes, Victor, the count, was striding toward him in the twilight and deepening shadows.

"Jonathan! What a surprise to find you here," boomed the rich baritone of the count. He now stood side by side with Jonathan.

Jonathan knew, beyond a shadow of suspicion, that the count had known exactly where to find him. The nightmarish journey, the horrid time in the castle all came back to him in a flash, and he stood rooted to the spot. It was as if a horrid nightmare had come to life and was now facing him.

He tried to speak, but his words caught in his throat. Victor turned to Lucy.

"And who is this marvelous, lovely woman?" he asked.

"M-Miss Lucy Westenra, m-meet Count Victor of Transylvannia," said Jonathan.

Victor swiftly took Lucy's hand and kissed it. As he did, he looked at her and said, "I am absolutely delighted to meet you, Miss Westenra."

Lucy giggled softly. "A *count*," she breathed. "I return the feeling."

Victor surveyed Lucy's town home. "Is this where you live?" he asked.

Go to the deuce! Jonathan wanted to shout. As it was, he could barely breathe.

"Indeed," said Lucy.

"Then I may make the pleasure of stopping by your lovely home in the future," he said.

"Please do," said Lucy. It sounded as though she were having trouble breathing, but for an entirely different reason.

The count nodded, and said, "Jonathan," and strode off into the night.

Turning to Jonathan, Lucy said, "A count! Do you think that counts own very much land in Transylvania? Jonathan?"

But Jonathan had fainted.

Chapter 10

The building was grand, as all buildings were in this towering, splendid, smelly city. Everywhere, it seemed as though there was a building trying to reach into the heavens, their heights soaring as far as man's hopes. Perhaps I would enjoy becoming lost in the city's depths after I dispatched Victor.

My shoes click-clacked on the cobblestones that made up the city streets, so different than the soft earth of the unpaved roads in the village in the mountains. I had to push my way past filthy street urchins begging for coins, (I tossed a few their way, just to get them out of my way) men shouting the news and trying to foist the daily paper into my hands, and pickpockets, silent, as far as humans went. But when one tried to reach into my dress to feel for a purse, I grabbed his hand in the blink of an eye, whirled around, and bared my teeth at him. He ran off, whimpering.

There was so much to take in, so much of a new city that I found, admittedly, overwhelming. The stench of London seemed to follow me everywhere I went, even when I walked by florists, with their buckets of flowers spilling into the streets, the soft blooms billowing their sweet fragrance into the air. When I traveled along the docks, fishmongers hollered their prices, and the salty tang of fish coated the back of my throat, and I knew that I would have to feed soon.

What truly astounded, was the sheer amount of *people* living in one place. My mouth watered at the prospect.

I arrived at the building the dockside whore told me about. Briefly, I surveyed the area, taking note of anyone going in or out of the building. None of them looked like Victor. Pausing in the street across from the famous house of flesh, I watched both men, and occasionally women on the arms of some man, enter. Everyone was dressed in their finery, the women wearing long robes of flowing fabric. I took in my own worn and tattered clothing, travel-stained and utterly shabby by comparison. Knowing how preoccupied humans are with their clothing, I went in search of something more appropriate.

Trancing a poor shop woman took little effort. Soon I was outfitted in a flowing dress with bare arms, a low V, and ruffles along my shoulders and collarbones. I could have done without the ruffles, but the midnight purple color suited me. It was the color of bruises and plum wine and set off my silky black hair nicely.

As I passed by a jewler's shop, I glanced at a string of black diamonds in the window.

Perfect, I thought.

In less time than it took the bell over the door to tinkle, I had charmed the necklace and matching earrings out of the storeowner's hands and onto my throat. The necklace was a choker and the earrings dangled so low that they brushed my neck.

I strode up to the building with confidence, sure of my disguise and conviction that waiting behind these doors was Victor. I rapped on the door in a velvet-gloved hand.

Someone opened a slit at eye-level.

"Password," the voice said.

I told it.

A pause.

"We do not take independent women," said the voice. "You must have a gentleman accompanying you."

Gods graces, just let me inside.

"Not even if I am to enjoy the pleasures of this house?" I purred.

The eye slit slammed shut.

I banged on the door with my fist.

"I am the new woman," I said, the lie rolling easily off my tongue. I couldn't very well put this human in a trance if I did not have eye contact.

The eye slit slid open again. An eye raked over my appearance.

"You're a spitfire. Jaqueline will have her hands full with you," said the male.

The door opened.

Inside, I was greeted by a sea of plush crimson and soft candlelight. I went from the inky, sharp blackness of the night to soft contours of cherry wood furniture, lush bowls of grapes and goblets of wine, and candles dripping with wax. I could hear the soft melody of a piano and raucous laughter coming from a large living area to my left. In front of me, a huge, straight staircase lined in red carpet led to the upper floors.

Everything about this place was saturated in luxury. Crystal chandeliers hung from the ceiling, marble fireplaces contained crackling flames, and the carpets lining the hardwood floors looked as though they came from the Orient. Men in evening suits wore pocket watches of gold and strode about with a woman, or two, on his arm. Paintings of nude women in various states of undress lined the walls, and I admired the artful rendering of pink, puckering nipples and indulgent lines of sensual grace. Even the accents of the guests were the clipped, refined speech of those who grew up with silver spoons in their mouths. It was not the drawling, loose speech of the woman at the docks.

A young woman who reminded me a bit of Berenice walked up to me. "You must be the new girl," she said.

"Yes, I am waiting for someone," I responded.

"What does he look like?" she asked.

"Tall, with eyes like nightshade, black hair to match, and pale skin. The lines of his face are rugged, hard, and exquisitely proportioned. His nose is somewhat hooked, but his square jaw balances it nicely. He is probably the most handsome man you have ever seen in your life."

The woman nodded, smiling a bit to herself. "Yes, that is the man Jaqueline meant for you to take. He is waiting for you upstairs. I will take you to the room." She must have been a coordinator of sorts; she did not look as though she sold herself night after night. Her face lacked the haunted look of most of the women here.

My heart began to beat faster as we made our way up the stairs. As we passed by room after room, cries of passion and lust filtered through the doorways. The long hallway seemed as dark as my dreams, and the I wondered how it would feel to finally sink my teeth into Victor's veins and drain him dry. There would be no mercy, no second guesses. I was ready to dispatch him. I could feel my predator's body tensing up in anticipation of the kill.

"Here is the room," the angel in front of me said. I would have loved to ravage her body; some other day, perhaps. She walked away, and I appreciated the sensuous lines of her body. "Goodnight."

Indeed, it would be a very good night. My hand paused on the doorknob, and I took a deep breath. I listened through the doorway. I heard a shift, the squeak of the mattress, and I knew that Victor was sitting on it. I could just imagine him: his tall, muscular torso twisting around as I entered, the look of shock on his face a split second before I sank my fangs into him, and the light draining from his eyes.

In one fluid motion, I twisted the knob, opened the door, and sprang into the room.

And I wrapped my hands around the throat of someone who was certainly not Victor.

Chapter 11

Consumed by hatred, forged by anger, my fingers squeezed of their own accord, and I watched the man's face before me slowly turn white. My whole body was on top of him, my legs straddling him on either side, as he lay prone on his back on the enormous bed. He weakly tried to scratch at my hands with his, but my grip was iron. It was only when I took stock of his features that I realized that his man was not Victor.

I released him, and he began to choke, gasping for air, but I did not move from his body. As the man drew weak breaths, I noticed how similar he looked to Victor, but there was something missing about him. He did not have the look of the preternatural; he was stunningly gorgeous, that was certain, like all those statues I had passed in my travels of angels. Indeed, I loved how his broad mouth opened as it pulled the air, his dark eyes wide and graced with delicate lashes. Something about the similarity between him and Victor made my body stand at attention.

"Madame," he said, still panting, eyes closed. "I do not know which other clients you have had and their unique proclivities, but I can assure you strangulation is not one of mine."

Damnation. This was a customer of this lovely establishment, which meant he was expected to pay, which meant that I could not kill him, lest the owner come looking for him.

He opened his eyes and looked at me. It was like falling upwards into a liquid sky of stars. The world seemed to tilt under me, and I did not like it. Not one bit. If Victor's gaze was piercing, this man, this handsome, exquisitely-carved mortal's was enveloping. I could get lost if I strayed too far.

I leapt off of him, as though I had been burned, turning around and looking over the room, to get my bearings. Then, I whirled around, my dress swishing behind me.

"Who are you?" I demanded. My body was still primed for fighting, for killing. My fangs ached to extend, but I kept them in, lest this human suspect anything, and do something foolish like start screaming.

Humans usually screamed.

The man sat up, rubbing his throat. "Quincy Morris, if it please you," he said. "May I ask the same of you?"

He looked at me, at my body, dragging his gaze from my feet to my head. I could see his eyes scrape over the fabric that clung to my curves, the dip of the V in my dress and the way it accentuated my full, high breasts.

"Amelia," I said.

"Amelia...?"

"Just Amelia."

The man—Quincy—nodded and said, "I understand. I suppose you usually don't give your last name to...clients."

"I don't work here," I said. "I was...looking for someone."

He peered at me, then as though taking stock of something that did not quite fit into a box. Of course, I did not.

"I see," he said, although he did not. Not truly, but those polished, London manners were taking over for him. He rose up from the bed, and my body tensed. Was he going to try to kill me, in return for trying to kill him? Was he going to run?

No. He simply strode over to me and took the decanter of wine from the table in front of me. He was so close now that I could smell him, fresh cotton and a spicy undertone, like bergamot. His aroma drifted around me, and my thirst sharpened to taste his blood.

"Who are you looking for?" he asked, as he poured two glasses of wine. The long-dormant human in me relished the squeak of the twisting cork, the clink of the bottle on the rim of the glass, the splash of liquid as it filled the cup.

He proffered one to me, and I took it. As a vampire, I could taste human food, but I hardly ate or drank it. Still, I enjoyed wine every now and then. Pinching the slender vine of crystal between my fingers, I lifted the glass to my nose and inhaled the aroma of cherries and chocolate. The memory of both triggered something deep within me.

The memory of summer, of feeling hot light on my skin.

The memory of the sun. Laughing through fields of wildflowers. Of happiness.

Something twisted in me, some deep, frozen part relaxed. I drank, feeling blood tears rise to my eyes.

"Someone who hurt me," I said, after drinking deeply. I held out the glass for him to refill; I had drunk it all entirely.

His was still half-full. Quincy eyed me, a question on his lips, but he did not ask. He simply poured and said, "I am here for the same reason."

Arching my eyebrow, I looked at him from over the rim of the glass, taking note of his broad shoulders, the sweep of his dark hair back from his face.

"And what will you do when you find this person?" he asked.

"Kill him," I replied.

Quincy laughed. "Do you really have that much confidence in your ability to bed a man? The French do say it is *la petit mort*." He polished off his glass, and I saw his body start to sway from the effects of the alcohol.

"Except his will not be little," I said. "It will be slow, grand, and excruciating."

"Sounds...titillating." He glanced from my face to my breasts and my nipples hardened.

"Yes," I responded. "I will get much pleasure from it."

Turning away, I walked to the window. I did not want to meet this man's gaze. He looked at me as though I were something fascinating, not as Victor did as something to control. I was not sure why the feeling produce discomfort in me, but it did. "Why are you here?" I asked the window. I could see his reflection in the glass; mine was absent. He did not notice. "Why did you come to this place?"

From the corner of my eye, I thought I saw a flash at the window. I ignored it and turned my attention back to the beautiful man before me.

Quincy filled his glass again. "Stupidity, really," he said.

I waited for him to continue. I knew that humans were dumb, but it was surprising to hear one admit it.

"I fancied myself in love," he continued. "I came here to drown my sorrows in sweet wine and sweeter flesh. The woman I love turned down my proposal of marriage. I came here to be distracted."

This time it was he who did not meet my gaze. I turned around.

"No, you didn't," I said, he moved his chin to the side, a masculine show of curiosity. I peered at him. "Perhaps that's one reason why you came, but not all."

He sighed, a soft huff of air escaping his lungs. "You are quite direct," he said, escaping the topic for a moment. "Most society girls will talk themselves around in circles without broaching a topic." He paused. "I suppose...I was embarrassed. More than embarrassed. I was humiliated. I came to her with my heart pouring out of me, and she dismissed me like a servant. I was ready to spend my life with her, but she does not return my affections, and I was abjectly mortified that I could have read her intentions so wrong."

He walked over to me. When he looked at me, I felt a soft, sinking feeling, as though I were being covered by a heavy blanket. It was not unpleasant. "I wanted to feel the admiration from someone. I wanted...intimacy. Even if it were fake. Even if it was only for a night."

This man surprised me with his truth. I was not sure if Victor had ever been truthful with me. It caught me off guard, and I did not know what to say.

I looked at him, this handsome man who looked so much like my paramour, my idol, my abomination. My belly clenched and suddenly, I knew my decision had been made.

"So here we are, two people with broken hearts, drinking wine, and lamenting the decisions that led us here," I said as I sauntered over to the bed. Gently, I lowered myself onto it and felt the lightness and airiness of the mattress. "However shall we get over this immense pain that we feel?"

Quincy's eyes narrowed to a keen point. I heard his heart begin to beat faster. I could almost see his thoughts as they turned around in his head: me, naked, on the bed. Him, ravishing me.

With as much nonchalance as I, he set down his glass on the small table and walked over. He stood before me and then placed two hands on either side of me, hemming me in. I smelled his aroma, sweet sunshine and grass. Nothing at all like Victor.

"A marvelous question. There are so many options," he murmured. He leaned down, his lips close to my ear. "We could go for a stroll in the park."

"There are thieves," I said, as he lifted a hand to my shoulder. He eased down the strap of my dress.

"We could take coffee in one of the nearby shops."

My breasts began to feel heavy within my dress. "I hate coffee."

He lowered my other strap.

"We could break into Buckingham palace," he murmured as he placed small kisses along my collarbone.

My skin tingled at his touch. His strong fingers began to unlace the back of my dress.

"Too many guards."

He paused, reveling in the moment before the storm. His mouth hovered over mine.

"Well then," he said, staring at my full lips, the exposed curve of my breast over the loosened dress. "I am all out of ideas."

And then he bent to kiss me.

Chapter 12

But his lips never touched mine. A different kind of tingling started along my skin. I looked sharply at the window.

Daylight! Dawn was almost breaking over the earth. I needed to find a place to sleep for the day.

Turning away my head, I said, "I have to go," and I quickly rose from the bed. My fingers reached around and tugged my laces into submission, and I fixed my dress sleeves back into place.

"Wha—" I was already at the door by the time Quincy had time to react. "Are you sure? You don't have to go. I was just—" he gestured to the bed in a helpless wave of his arm. "We don't have to do anything."

"I know. I still have to go."

And with those words, I left, shutting the door against his saddened, quizzical expression. Racing through the streets of London, I found an old crypt on the outskirts of the city. Some part of me still wondered if I could be immune from the sunlight, but I did not want to take a chance on dying while Victor still lived. As I lay myself down on the cold stone, my last thought was not of Victor, but of Quincy, of his strong hands, his open face that betrayed all of his emotions, and...his truth. It was as though he had opened himself up like a book for me to read. As I closed my eyes, I found it curious that I wanted to read more.

The next night, I sprang up, eager to renew my hunt for Victor. Prowling along the streets of the city, I found no end to humans whose blood I could drink on a whim. There were so many people that one less beggar would not be missed.

My target was filthy, his clothes in rags. His beard was unkempt and crawling with lice. He was aimlessly wandering, muttering to himself. I came up behind him, ready to drag him deep into a dark alley.

Then, he turned. When he saw my face, he exclaimed, "It's you!"

I kept my face very still. How on earth did this beggar seem to know me?

"I've seen you before," he said, giggling slightly. "He sends me pictures, and I can see the pictures here." He brought a finger to his temple and touched. "You're there sometimes, yes, I recognize you from his pictures."

There was only one being I knew who could send mental pictures into the minds of humans. My mind began to churn at an alarming rate. This man was my key, my compass. I took him by the shoulders and shook.

"Do you know where he is?" I asked.

"Oh it's nice to live by the bay, by the bay, by the bay," replied the man in a sing-song voice.

I shook him harder. "Where is he?"

The man looked at me and laughed. "He is found when he wants to be found." He held up a finger and wagged it slowly back and forth. "And not before."

This maddening creature would force me to break his legs if he did not start speaking with sense.

"You're right, you're right," I said, releasing my hold on him, even though my fingers were still curled, and my jaw was clenched. "What are the images you've seen? What has he sent you?"

The man began to amble down the road, and I followed him. The other passers-by of the city gave us a wide berth, more for the smell emanating from the man's body than anything else.

"Oh, the master sends many things, yes, many pictures. Castles and sheep, women and blood," he said, spreading his arms out wide for no reason at all.

Castles. Sheep. That would be our home, deep in the Carpathian mountains.

"And the master knows where to sleep for the night. The master is smart," he continued. "The church, yes, the church with the angels guarding it. They will never look for him there!" And the man began to guffaw, great, wrenching pangs of laughter.

The church. I knew the one. It was hemmed by statues of angels, guarding the door. It looked like the entrance to heaven.

"The master calls to me," I said, tearing away from the man.

As I ran down the streets, my mind teetered with questions. What on earth had Victor to do with some raggedy man who could not hold two sequential thoughts in his mind? What use had he at all?

This particular mystery would have to wait. Or I might never find out. I did not care. All I could see in front of me was the cobblestones, leading like arrows to the church.

I had to admit, it was rather brilliant of Victor to hide in a church. For centuries, people had whispered that we could not enter churches, that we were damned, and as such, we would explode into flame upon entering, or that water blessed by priests would burn us, or a thousand other tiresome myths.

This was, of course, not the case.

As my feet drew me nearer, I swallowed. This would be it. I could feel his presence getting stronger. One does not live five hundred years with someone and not know what they feel like, their ripple in the ever-swirling current of life.

I walked up the steps of the church. Pried open the door.

There, Victor stood, as though waiting for me.

Chapter 13

Moonbeams of light sliced through the air in the church. It was an old building, and there was no glass on the windows, only an open space. This city was beginning to fascinate me, with its mix of old and new, decrepit, and pristine. The air around us hung low and heavy, smelling of must, mold, and dead things. Rain began pattering outside, and soon, the air turned clean, settling all the dust and debris of the city.

Victor smiled. "I knew that you would find me here," he said.

My heart, if I had a heart, pounded. It was a relic of things long past, sort of like humans when they suffer a limb chopped off and they still feel phantom pain. My heart still experienced phantom beats.

I did not return the smile.

"You lied," I said.

My god, he looked so good in the moonlight. His shoulders still held that width that I loved. He was tall, and his black hair seemed a perfect foil to the moonlight. Of course, he would still look the same; we had been separate mere days, bu to me, it felt like a lifetime. I realized that I head expected him to look different, warped, somehow less than perfectly attractive, but he was not. All he wonderful lines were still straight, his fangs still sharp. His slow smile still had that cat-like charm to it, and all I wanted to do was wrap my arms around him. Whether to strangle or to embrace, I did not know quite yet. I was sure my mind would figure it out at any moment. For a second, he reminded me of Quincy, not the other way around. I shook my head.

"Why did you lie?" I asked, stepping toward him. There was a huge bible laid out on a podium, and statues of Mary and Jesus hung all around us. I thought that they would judge me at first, with their sorrowful eyes, but then I realized that they had better things to do than worry about a lover's quarrel. I even thought that Mary might understand me. She must have known what it was like to love a man so deeply, then have to let him go.

He knew what I meant. Still, he shrugged the question off, as though rolling a stone off him. He replied with one of his own.

"How did you travel here?"

My anger flared. I could tell he was subtly trying to change the conversation, to steer it in a way that suited him. Well, I knew what he was doing, and I reared my whole being against being manipulated.

"With my feet. Now: why did you lie? Why did you say that I would die if I crossed the boundary of my land and the others?" I demanded. I had to know. Please let there be a good reason that my wonderful Victor, my companion through the ages saw fit to deceive me for so long.

For the briefest second, Victor glanced sideways. "I wanted to keep you safe," he said.

"Safe from what?" I took another step.

Victor took a step backward, and I thought the Armageddon the Christians talked about had come. Victor never gave ground for anything.

"There are...things that are difficult to explain," he said, his throat bobbing. "And I know you came here with your feet, you cheeky minx. How specifically?"

The thought that Victor cared for my safety, even if I were an immortal vampire, soothed the raging ache in me for a moment, so I answered.

"I stole some maps from a peasant and made the overland trail. I hid during the day in underground shelters. It was not that difficult,"

I added, my pride flaring out like a peacock's feathers. "And you?" My whole body was attuned to his answer. He was a tuning fork, and I was his instrument.

"The seas. I was stored in the cargo bin, with coffins of earth from our country," he said. I was able to travel during the day, and at night, I picked off passengers at my leisure. They thought it was the plague."

I nodded; none of this mattered. It was only a way to deflect from what was happening before my eyes. Victor was changing; he had already changed.

That, to me, felt like he had died.

He must have seen my face fall, because in a moment, he was standing beside me, gently caressing my cheek.

"Shhhh, do not worry," he said. "It will all turn out right."

Suddenly, all my anger fled. Some of Mary's sadness must have seeped into me via the moonbeams, for I was suddenly exhausted with it. I leaned my head forward and rested it against Victor's chest. He cupped his hand against the back of my head and gently rubbed. It felt so good that prickles arose on my flesh.

"Why are you leaving us?" I whispered into the cloth of his shirt. "I am losing you."

"But I haven't gone anywhere," he said, smiling, his fangs exposed. My loins stirred at the sight of those elongated teeth. "I am right here with you."

"Just come back," I said. I hated begging, but here I was, pleading with him yet again. "Just come back home to us. We need you."

"But the world needs me more!"

He broke away from me, and spread out his hands, as though to embrace the church. He walked a couple of steps forward, toward the door, away from Mary clutching her heart. The moonlight illuminated his face, smiling with grand dreams. Suddenly, he spun on his heel to face me.

"Don't you see the beauty of it? Humans are becoming more and more numerous. Gone are the days where they would die by the thousands, by the millions, like this," and he snapped his fingers. "Now they have new medicine to keep them healthy. The poor no longer rot in the streets like they used to. They have hospitals and churches to help keep people living for longer."

"What of that to us?" I said acidly. "However long they live, human lives are but a heartbeat to ours."

"Think, Amelia! The longer they live, the longer they have a chance to reproduce. The more that they reproduce and not die, the more humans there will be populating the earth. I can feel it. They will become more and more numerous with time. It is already happening. Just this century alone, they are more than there ever were. And if there are more humans, it will be harder to hide. They *will* discover us."

I had not considered all that. My mind rebelled against the thought that Victor was right, but I could see the brutal logic to it.

"They will discover us and exterminate us, unless we have more of our kind. We need to make a larger family, to ensure our own survival."

"To hell with our own survival. Perhaps it is the way of the world to die one day. Perhaps we are only living on borrowed time—just more than the humans."

Victor suddenly sped toward me, towered over me. In a flash, his face changed from hopeful exuberance to rage.

"Don't you ever say that," he whispered. "Do not spit in the face of immortality."

That rage which used to scare me somehow did not anymore. I could not understand why, but I found that I could do something which I had never done.

I pushed Victor.

Putting both my hands on his chest, I pushed as hard as I could, saying, "Then don't spit on my love for you! You have left us like we were dirt!"

For a moment, Victor looked shocked, then he began laughing. The flames of my anger only rose higher as each peal echoed throughout the church rafters.

"You wicked creature! From whence comes this new passion?" He looked at me as though he suddenly wanted to bite me and hard.

My fangs lowered in response.

"Come and find out," I purred, lethal and ready.

He shot toward me. He grabbed my right arm, but I swung my left arm down in an attempt to break his. He let go, and I used my momentum to swing around and kick him. He caught my foot, which nearly threw my balance off, but I stayed steady.

With my free leg, I jumped and twisted, and I landed on top of his shoulders. He let go in shock, and I slid down him, wrapping my hands around his throat to strangle him. I should have used my arms.

He gripped my arms and threw me over his shoulder. Before I hit the ground on my back, I twisted and stuck one leg out and managed to find my balance.

Victor held me as though we were two dancers doing the modern dance of tango, and he leaned down and kissed me deeply.

I hit him in the head with my own, and blood started to trickle down his nose. I leaned forward and licked the trail that flowed down his mouth.

"You like to lick fluids?" he growled, enraged with passion and ire. "Try this."

I knew what he meant, but he would have to make me first.

I broke off, then ran to the altar, where a lit candelabra sat. Gripping the solid gold stem, I threw it at his head, candles and all.

The white candles flew through the air, their white wax dripping everywhere. The tiny flames petered in the air current, but they stayed lit. It was like watching death itself, terrifying and beautiful.

He dodged the candles, taking a few steps to the side, around the altar. He looked at me with huge eyes, and I realized that, perhaps for the first time in our lives, I had scared him. I knew that I had gone too far. That was not supposed to be a part of the game. One did not simply play with fire.

I tried to feel guilty, but I could not.

"That's. Not. Funny," he hissed through clenched teeth.

I tried to make a run for the side door. All at once, he was on me, dragging me back to the altar. He swept everything else off of it, bible, delicate lace cloth, holy water. It all went clattering to the floor.

He had one of my arms pinned behind me, and he forced my body over the table, as though he were about to enter me from behind. My arm hurt, but I said nothing.

"Submit."

Still, I said nothing. He pulled my arm up, and my tendons screamed for relief.

"I said submit," he whispered. "I do not want to do this."

Of course, you do, I thought. You live for this. You live for power. You thrive on it as much as you do the blood.

Neither my arm nor my heart could take any more.

"I submit," I said, and immediately, he released the pressure, but he did not release my arm.

"You know what to do," he whispered.

I did. And god help me, I wanted it. I wanted nothing more than to do what I did next, which was flip him over, so that he laid on his back on the table. I knew he had allowed me to do that. I could have only done it if he wanted.

I tugged at his pants and pulled them down. The length of him sprang free, as hard as I had ever seen it. My mouth wrapped around him, just as I hoped my heart wound around his.

This was so much more immediate and satisfying, though.

I sucked, with all the power that I had in me, deep pulls, and Victor groaned in response. I sucked, flicking my tongue over him, and it was not long before he reached the pinnacle of his pleasure, so aroused he was by our fight. My own body echoed the tremors.

When he was finished, he said, "If she is half as good as you are, she will make a good vampire." He re-fastened his pants.

Those words! It was as though a thousand demons sprang from hell and were now ripping my heart to shreds. I tried to remind myself that I did not have a heart.

It did no good.

I do not even remember leaving the church.

All I had in my mind was that I would kill whoever Victor had his sights set on. If there was no more girl, then there would be no one to join us. Victor would see it was useless to make the family grow. He would come back to us.

Or I would kill him.

Chapter 14

Quincy's head was spinning.

Who on earth had he met? She was unlike any other woman that he had known in his life. She was fierce, arrogant, diabolical, and seemed unconstrained by any societal convention. It was as though he had been trapped in a room full of snails, and suddenly a tiger walked through. The London Society girls were quaint, charming, very well-mannered, and utterly, completely, and mind-numbingly boring.

He did not think it was their fault, he supposed. After all, what can you do if you have been taught to wear a corset from the age of fourteen?

But still, have some interest in the world around you!

She was beautiful; there was no question about that. Her midnight hair had fallen so elegantly around her heart-shaped face, and her green eyes had pierced him. He had felt as though she could see into his very soul; he would not be surprised if she could. They were pale, her eyes, and looked like two emeralds that had gone too long without seeing the sun. That was not how emeralds worked, of course, but Quincy could not find a better analogy.

She had moved so graceful, like each movement was an extension of her. She walked with the utmost assurance that she was beautiful and (and Quincy was puzzled by this) deadly. He had seen the same posture on some of the members of Scotland Yard. It was the quiet strength of someone who does not need to brawl or get into tavern fights to show off their fortitude, as some blokes liked to on a Saturday night. No, it was the utter relaxed posture that gave it away, as though she could spring into action at any moment but chose to bide her time to strike.

He wanted to see her again.

No, he needed to see her again. He had so many questions. Where had she come from? Her accent was so lyrical; it was obvious that she was foreign. And because she was foreign, she had that lovely, exotic quality. Some of the speech she had used was quite old, and sometimes she sounded like a grandmother when she talked, but that only added to her mystery and allure. How did someone, who spoke like they lived in the past century, come to London's most famous brothel?

Quincy still had not solved the mystery the next night, when he set off looking for her. He had very little idea of where to look, so he started around the area where they had met. He looked rather quickly and did not stay in one place too long. This was the armpit of London. Stray dogs wandered around, scratching their mange and fleas; clothes hung on lines between windows, and Quincy frequently had to look up to avoid refuse being tossed out the windows. He heard a variety of languages that were certainly not English. The area was populated with prostitutes and pickpockets and worse, and Quincy wore his worse set of clothing to try to blend in.

After hours of fruitless searching, Quincy stood in a corner to try to get bearings. He tried to look up at the sky, to see which was the sun was in the sky, but the buildings were too high and too numerous.

He was lost.

Quincy took a long, slow breath and told himself to not be a ninny. He simply needed to find a main road that would lead him out of this dump. The only problem was that it was difficult to find any road through the twisting, turning side alleys. He tried to ask for directions once, but the old, hunchback woman started yelling at him angrily, and he took off running.

Something rose in his throat. He kept glancing out of the corner of his eye, sure that some evil character were stalking him, or about to plunge a knife into his side to steal his wallet, or knock him over the head...

And night was falling. In truth, it had already fallen, but Quincy did not want to admit that. His sweat froze on him.

Stepping into one of the tiny alleys, Quincy paused to catch his breath and to focus his mind. When he glanced up, he saw two figures across the alleyway from him, although they were deep in conversation. The younger man with dark black hair was tall, with exotic looking clothes, although he wore a suit, like a proper Englishman. The other appeared to be a doctor, with graying hair, spectacles, and a dark gray beard.

They were deep in conversation and did not notice Quincy. Quincy saw the younger man pass the older a knife and what looked to be like a very large sum of money. The older man kept glancing around, as though certain someone would sneak up on him. Quincy was certain that he should run, but his eyes were fixed on the transaction before his eyes. He knew that it was something awful. He knew that the younger man wanted the older man to do something awful for him and was willing to pay mountains for it. He shivered. He told himself to move, but his body did not respond.

Suddenly, the younger man looked right at him.

Quincy felt his bones freeze.

The dark, handsome man whispered something to the old man and bade him to go away with a flick of his white wrist.

Quincy blinked, and all of a sudden, the man was standing there before him.

"Good evening," the man said, his accent thick, but not undecipherable. "It's a bit late for you to be walking around this unsavory sector, isn't it?"

"Directions, my good man," he said. His heart was beating wildly, but he would not let it show. "All I need are directions to leave this, as you call it, 'unsavory sector.'"

The man looked at him long and hard. "Two streets up is 7th Avenue. Take it back to the main drag through this stinking, glorious city."

Quincy had no doubt if the man had had one knife, he might have more, and that he was more than capable of plunging it into his heart.

The man leaned forward, and Quincy leaned back out of instinct. The man closed his eyes and inhaled, as though smelling the air around Quincy.

"Yes, you're Amelia's new plaything. I saw you through the window. Good. She needs a distraction. That's the only reason why I'm letting you live," he said.

In a heartbeat, he was gone.

Quincy ran all the way to 7th street.

Chapter 15

When he opened the newspaper that morning, Quincy nearly lost all his breakfast. There, splattered in bloody glory, was the photo of a woman with her throat ripped out. It was ghastly and sensational, and London was eating it up. He folded down the paper, so he would not have to look at it.

At that moment, the doorbell rang. It was sure to be Dr. Seward, another one of Lucy's castaways. She had had three suitors. Three! Himself, Dr. Seward, and Arthur Holmwood, one of his best mates. He knew that he should feel happy for Arthur, but the embarrassment still stung. He had not told Arthur of his affections for Lucy until after their engagement had been announced. Lucy had looked so beautiful in the papers, not at all like the poor woman with matted, tangled hair and a gruesome slash across her throat. Quincy took the smallest comfort in that he knew Dr. Seward felt the same embarrassment of rejection.

We should form a club, thought Quincy. *A bitter hearts, two-person club.*

He shook himself. He was not usually this sour in the morning, but the image of the woman in the newspaper had burned into his mind, and he wanted to get it out.

"Good morning, doctor," said Quincy as he opened the door to a man with iron gray hair fading to white and a well-trimmed beard. "Let's make this quick. I have a very important meeting with someone today, and I cannot be late."

That was a bald lie, and Quincy prayed that he would not go to hell for it. The only thing on his mind was finding that woman he had met. It had been a week, and still he had not found any sign of her.

"Medicine cannot be rushed," said the doctor, in a clipped, vaguely Scottish voice. Although the doctor was British, he had studied medicine at the University of Edinburgh, and he said that the Scots accent had got into him and he had never shaken it since. "Alls well?"

"Yes, I just wanted to follow up with you, since...well, since that night," said Quincy. Quincy had called on Dr. Seward to take a look at him. Since the night in the dark alleyways of London, he had been experiencing horrible nightmares. Every night, a monster came down and slashed his throat and drank from him. He suspected it would be worse upon seeing the awful pictures in the news.

"And you, good doctor?"

"Oh fine, fine. Just working on a health serum, to fortify the senses and strength. How is your morning?"

"Well, I woke up to this rubbish."

Quincy passed Dr. Seward the paper.

Dr. Seward tutted. "Dreadful business, that. They're saying it's one person who is chopping up all those women," he said, as he listened to Quincy's heart. "No one can solve it. It's giving even that bloke on Baker Street a run for his money."

"I can't imagine how one person could do all that," replied Quincy. He blinked once the doctor had stopped looking into his eyes and made him follow his finger.

"Madman," replied Dr. Seward. "I know plenty of them. I have a patient, Renfield. Completely off his rocker. Mumbles to himself. Goes wandering the streets at night. He constantly escapes the asylum, and we have to go hunting for him." Dr. Seward paused. "I would not be surprised if it were him doing all this slashing."

Quincy straightened. "Really?" he said.

Dr. Seward tapped on Quincy's knee to test the reflex. "Most certainly."

Quincy suddenly had a horrible stomach cramp. "What does he look like?"

"What you would expect a madman to look like. Doesn't bathe. Hair scattered to the four winds. Graying." Dr. Seward shook his head. "We've been trying to catch him for days. Why? You haven't seen him, have you?"

Quincy remembered the cold eyes of the man he had seen in the dark alley. He had known him, knew who he was. He had said that he had seen Quincy, even. At that moment, he could not imagine revealing anything about what he had seen that night, even to his trusted friend.

Quincy shook his head. " 'Fraid not, old boy."

"Bother. Well, you seem in good condition. Not about to fall over from exhaustion. You probably just had a fright. It'll pass in a day or two. I can give you some laudanum to help you sleep, if you wish."

Quincy negated the offer. "It makes me too groggy the next morning."

"Right then," said Dr. Seward standing up. Once he was at the door, he turned and said, "Do let me know if you see anything suspicious. I am quite keen to catch Renfield before he hurts someone, if he hasn't already."

Quincy promised to do so, hating the dirty feeling of lying. He could have told the doctor what he had seen, but then he would have had to explain why he was in the alley in the first place, and even Quincy could not answer that particular question just then.

Chapter 16

After an entire morning of searching, Quincy decided to stop by his friend, Arthur Holmwood. A servant answered the bell.

"The Lord Holmwood is not presently in," a maid in a white bonnet said. "He has gone to the Miss Lucy Westenra's house."

Wonder why the old chap's over there, he thought.

Quincy thanked her and with needles in his heart, decided to visit. Arthur was not above visiting places of ill-repute, and he would have to get over the sight of Lucy someday.

Chin up, he told himself. You've faced worse than this before.

Upon ringing the doorbell, Arthur himself answered it. He looked like death on two legs.

"Quincy," said Arthur. His clothes were unkempt, and he had enormous, dark circles under his eyes. He looked as though he had aged ten years, since Quincy had last seen him, and that was only a week ago.

"Arthur—good god, what's happened? And where is Lucy?" His stomach clenched at the sight of Arthur. Whatever had happened, it was not good.

"Come inside and we'll speak."

Quincy stepped inside the familiar home, with its lavish decorations.

They stepped into the sitting room, and once again, Quincy felt a strange, surreal feeling overtake him. Only a few days ago had he sat in this same cushioned sofa, with his heart in his hands. Now, it beat wildly, anxious and uncertain.

"What's happened?" asked Quincy.

Arthur sighed deeply before speaking. "I do not know whether to tell you the worst news of my life or the best. Even the best is tinged with sadness."

"I find that life is a little less bleak when news ends on a positive note."

"Very well. My—" Arthur cleared his throat. Quincy saw that he was struggling not to cry. "My father is dead."

Quincy's eyebrows raised toward his hairline. "But he was young still. What happened?"

Arthur's fist clenched against his knee. "Murdered."

Quincy gasped. "What? By whom?"

Arthur rubbed his face with his hand. "That's the devil of it. We don't know yet. He was found with a knife plunged in his heart—and that's it."

Quincy's stomach roiled. "Do you think it's connected with those women? Had he any enemies?"

Arthur merely shook his head slowly. "I don't know. I don't know anything anymore. My world is spinning."

So was Quincy's mind. Who on earth would want to kill Arthur's father?

So that's why the maid addressed Arthur as "Lord Holmwood," Quincy thought bleakly.

He cleared his throat. "Well, tell me your good news. You said it was the best you could receive."

Arthur sighed and shook himself. "Well, yes. I asked Lucy for her hand in marriage—and she accepted."

Quincy could not help the twinge of jealousy that wracked his heart; immediately, he felt guilty of being jealous of a man whose father had just been murdered.

"That's—that's wonderful," said Quincy. "Congratulations. I am sure you will be very happy together."

Arthur smiled softly. "Yes, but the thing is—she's sick, Quincy. Dreadfully so. She's turned pale and has no appetite. Her servants have tried plying her with food and drink, but she will take nothing. Sometimes a bit of broth."

It was then that Quincy's stomach plummeted. "Sick? With what?"

Arthur's shoulders raised a fraction of an inch. "Who can say? Dr. Seward has been over a half a dozen times, and he has no idea what ails her. He said that his new serum may help her eventually, but he is still experimenting with it."

Quincy nodded. "May I see her?"

"Of course."

The two men rose from the couch and went into Lucy's bedroom, where a servant was standing at attention. The room was cast in darkness, and only a few candles burned.

My god, she looks awful, thought Quincy.

Lucy's face was as white as the roses that stood on her boudoir. Her cheeks were drawn, and her lips were a pale beige.

Upon entering, she lifted her head a fraction of an inch off the pillow. Her normally radiant hair was dull and straw-like.

"Quincy darling," she murmured. "How good of you to come."

Quincy approached her. "Of course, my dear." He gave her a kiss on the forehead. Then, looking around the room, he said, "It is awfully dark in here. Wouldn't you rather draw back the curtains and let in fresh air and sunlight? It might do you good."

"No, no," said Lucy, reaching for his hand and giving it a weak squeeze. "The sunlight hurts my head so. I can barely stand it as it is."

Quincy tried to swallow the lump in his throat. "Rest now. You'll get better soon."

But she had already fallen asleep.

The maid knocked on the door. "Sirs? Dr. Seward is here to check on Miss Lucy."

Arthur turned to Quincy. "Speak of the devil, eh?"

Dr. Seward entered, with deep circles under his eyes.

"Doctor, you look about as bad as Miss Lucy," said Quincy. "Are you all right?"

"Fine, fine," said the doctor, brushing off his friend's concern. "Only staying up late at night, working on my serum, and trying to find a cure for Miss Lucy." His eyes quickly scanned over her pale face. "We'll need to give her an injection of blood."

Arthur immediately stepped forward, but the doctor shook his head. "No, you've already given too much these past few days. I'm worried enough as it is." He turned to Quincy. "Would you be willing?"

"Of course," said Quincy, already drawing back his sleeve.

Lucy moaned a little from the sheets. "He calls to me," she whispered. "I must go."

"There, there, my love, it will be all right," said Arthur, as Dr. Seward readied the medical equipment.

When the blood transfusion was complete, Arthur and Quincy stepped outside the room, leaving Dr. Seward alone with Lucy.

Quincy did not know what to say at first. He ran a hand through his hair and said, "She'll recover. Whatever this mysterious illness is, Dr. Seward will know what to do."

Arthur only looked at Quincy and murmured, "I hope to God that you're right."

Chapter 17

I felt as though my world had tilted or that I had been set out to sea in a small boat, just drifting. I did not know who to be or how to feel without Victor. In a futile attempt to get him off my mind, I thought of the man, Quincy. He was cocky; I liked that. He seemed confident and that titillated something inside me. I had wanted to bed him just for a distraction, just to get Victor out of my head for five minutes.

When I had seen Victor, I couldn't do it. I could not kill him as I had wanted to. I wanted to preserve our family, not tear it apart, and if I killed Victor, then I would be just as much of a monster as he was. So instead, I focused on finding his first human target.

She, and it would be a she, would be fair-toned. Even if he had not mentioned it, I knew that he would target a young, beautiful woman. I had a rough idea of what she would look like, too. Victor already had a dark beauty, me; a red-haired goddess, and a cinnamon-brown one. He would now look for someone with golden tones, a blond-haired-blue-eyed damsel to add to his growing rainbow.

I tried tracking Victor for several days, without luck. He would always slip away into the shadows, and I had a hard time finding this mystery woman.

One night, Victor appeared before me.

"You're not going to find her, so you might as well stop looking," he said.

"Well now I have to find her," I responded. "You said not to, so here we are."

Victor groaned, the sound vibrating my belly. "Amelia, just accept that this is for the best." He glanced over my shoulder. "And it looks like your plaything is here."

I turned. Quincy!

"Have fun," whispered Victor as he casually strolled away.

Quincy strode up like he had the hounds of hell after him but was trying to maintain the guise of being an English gentleman.

"Amelia!" he whispered, grabbing my arm and pulling me away. "What are you doing here?" He cast a furtive glance behind us, his eyes scanning for signs of Victor.

"Talking to... an old friend," I said. 'Lover' did not come close, and I did not believe in soul mates.

I was not sure that I still had a soul.

We walked toward the docks. The moon had risen, and the water lapped at the ships' hulls, making a soothing, gentle sound.

"I do not know your business with that...gentleman, and I know that it may be presumptuous of me to say, but...you should not talk to him," said Quincy. Now that we were out of the alleyways, we walked at a slower pace. "The man does not give an impression of trustworthiness." If the words had been stiffer, they would have been corpses in the ground.

I admit, I felt the tiniest bit of warmth from someone caring about me. I had not realized that someone could care about my well-being. It was new; after hundreds of years of immortality, one got accustomed to being impervious to pain, suffering, disease, and death. The notion that someone had thought about my safety was both quaint and...endearing. This new feeling sparked a tiny ember in me.

It was only then that I realized that Quincy still had his arm around mine, and that we were walking arm in arm down the docks. I did not pull away.

"Quincy, I thank you for your kindness, but I am more than capable of taking care of myself," I said.

He crinkled his mouth. "But that fellow...I know he is evil. I can feel it. I cannot explain it, but I know he is," he said. "He does not have the best intentions with you."

I laughed. "Nor I with him," I said. "Quincy, if you knew who I really was, you would go screaming off into the night. You would never have anything to do with me again."

He shook his head. "Never. You are far too clever to abandon."

The gods must have been listening that night, for they sent me the perfect opportunity to prove him wrong. Perhaps fate would have intervened in any case, but it was right at that moment that I saw figures descending a gangplank of a ship.

What caught my attention was that they were too short to be adult. Tiny little waifs were walking on unsteady legs down the rough, wooden boards of the bridge between ship and solid ground. Once they had settled, there were about five or six of them, I saw them surround a man. The man had a belly hanging over his belt and a whip at his side.

Instantly, my body became wired. It seemed that nothing had changed in five hundred years. Whips were still used to enslave.

The wind pushed back the cloaks of the children, and I saw they were girls, every one. Some already had their faces painted, looking garish and hideous in the moonlight. They were all beautiful.

When I saw the man exchange money with another man, something in me snapped. I did not care about humans. Humans were food, my sustenance. Every human, no matter what, had lived long enough to do something wicked, and I felt not one shred of guilt sucking them dry.

But these were children. They had not lived long enough to decide right from wrong.

Innocence, I thought, and a lump formed in my throat, just as my hand curled into a fist.

I whirled to face Quincy. "You want to see who I really am? Fine. Follow if you must, but keep silent, and don't let them see you," I said.

"Who? Those men over there?"

"I said keep silent! And don't point, for godssake."

I slunk into the night.

The first man walked away and darted into an adjoining alley. I would deal with him first.

I came up behind him and snapped his neck, a merciful death, one that he did not deserve. He did not even see it coming.

Quickly, I followed the scent of the other man, which was not hard to do, considering the odor of rotting onions and goat's breath was as evident as a lighthouse.

He stopped in front of a decrepit building with a red lamp hanging outside of it. It was another tavern of flesh, although one of much lesser quality than the one I had first met Quincy in.

I stepped into a pool of light made by a gas lamp. Keeping my fangs in check, I did not want to needlessly scare the children. It was for their sake that I gave the second man a chance. They were probably already plagued with plenty of nightmares. I did not want to give them more by killing a man in front of them.

Even though they might have already seen worse, I thought.

"Let them go," I said.

The man whipped around at the sound of my voice.

"Lady, this don't concern you none," said the gelatinous cretin. He began to turn back around and raise his fist to the door.

"Let them go, and I will let you live," I replied. My words were sharper than a blade, and the girls' eyes went wide at them. They, at six and seven years of age, had more sense than this bubbling mass of golem in front of me.

The man laughed and turned around again. "What's that, then? You taking the piss out of me?"

"Let. Them. Go."

The man's smile instantly left him. Slowly, he withdrew a knife.

"My little friend here says it's time for you to walk along, now," the man said.

The girls drew in a breath at the same time. I turned to them and said, "Close your eyes."

Most of them did. One kept hers open. I swear I saw myself reflected in her brown eyes.

I took a step forward, and the man lunged. He had some skill with the blade, I'll give him that. He swiped, but I easily side-stepped him.

He cut across, and when he did, I slammed my forearm down on his, breaking it. The knife clattered against pavement stones.

The man howled in pain, and I punched him across the jaw. He fell down, hard, and I knew that his vision must have blurred with the impact. For a moment, I saw a pair of eyes through a slit in the door, but when I looked up, the tiny slit quickly shut at the sight of a knife. No one wanted to be a witness to a murder or alley fight. The less Scotland Yard came sniffing around looking for answers, the better business was.

With one hand, I gripped the edge of his shirt and pulled. The bloated individual must have weighed at least two hundred and fifty pounds, but I dragged him like he was a string. I could have carried him, but I wanted the pavement to scrape against his bare skin.

I pulled him into an adjoining alley. With the knife, I quickly slashed his throat, making it look like what it was: an alley fight that he lost. If I drained him, there would be too many questions. Blood splattered against my dress.

When I looked up, Quincy was staring at me, his expression a profound mix of horror, curiosity, and puzzlement.

Standing up, I let the knife drop to the ground. I did not need it.

To my utter surprise, Quincy walked forward and picked it up. "This is a steel blade worth at least fifty pounds sterling," he said. He cleaned it, took the sheath from the dead man, and slid it back into the case. He tried to give it to me.

"Keep it," I said. "I have no use for it."

"Of course," Quincy whispered, as if it were the most obvious thing in the world.

Wordlessly, I walked back to the door, where the children were still standing. I waved my hand at them.

"Come," I said, motioning with my hand. Just as I had no use for a knife, I had little and less to do with children. Just because I wanted to preserve whatever innocence they had left did not mean I wanted to maintain a gaggle of them.

The little girl who had kept her eyes open stepped forward first. She took the hand of the girl behind her, then one by one they all did the same.

We went through the alleys, Quincy bringing up the rear of our little gang. I stopped them at a church and banged on the door until someone answered.

"Take them," I said and walked away.

I did not notice Quincy slip a very large sum of money into the poor nun's hands.

Quincy did not say anything for a very long time. He kept opening his mouth and inhaling, as though on the very edge of saying something, but he did not.

Finally, when we had returned to the docks, he turned to me.

"What are you?" he said.

In that moment, I could have lied. I could have said any number of things or simply vanished. But Quincy drew me. He had not gone screaming into the night, as I had imagined he would. And though he had looked on in horror, his face had lacked disgust. If he had been disgusted, I could not have supported him.

But he didn't. He stayed. Perhaps he wanted to help the children as well.

I think the greatest reason why I told him the truth was because he knew that I was not human immediately. I was beginning to realize that Quincy felt things deeply, sensed things that he could not explain logically, unlike any human I had ever known. He had asked what I was, not who. With that, I opened my mouth to speak.

"I am a vampire."

Chapter 18

We stared at each other for an innumerable amount of time. Years, eternities, flashing before us. I wondered how this human was going to react, which was he was going to jump. Would he panic, try to kill me?

He swallowed. I could hear his heart beating furiously beneath his ribs. Part of me longed to sink my fangs into him, draw out that rich ichor that pumped in his veins, but I held still. Even now, I cannot say for certain what stayed my hand and did not end his life. Was it the way he looked at me, with curiosity and fascination and not terror? Was it the way he kept his back and shoulders straight, as if to say, "If I must meet death here, let it come?"

Such trivialities are past us now.

He swallowed. Then spoke. "So?"

My god, this man would have grown taller if not for the weight of his balls.

I smirked. Fine. If he wanted to stare death in the face, then let us dance to that tune. He would scream eventually.

"Come," I said. Jerking my head in the direction of the lovely but hideous brothel, I turned without bothering to see if he followed. "If we must speak, I prefer to do it in suitable conditions. If you have the constitution to listen, then you must have a very strong appetite for what is to follow."

I made my way through the filthy streets. Truly, this must be the bowels of hell, with streets filled with horse dung and urine, trash and rubbish in the river, and the thick, greasy taste of fog coating the backs of our throats. Evil lived here, even wretched wicked than I. I could sense it hiding among the billowing fog that crept into every crevice and niche.

When I glanced behind me, Quincy followed. I knew he would. I could feel us tied together, like the filament between two wires on a lightbulb, that wonderous invention of Edison's.

I already had what I needed. Prowling the streets of London gave me the insight into all the rich and vile pleasures that this city had to offer. We simply needed privacy. What better place for privacy than a brothel?

We entered, and I placed a fair amount of gold into the young woman's hands. "For the night," I said.

Taking Quincy's hand, I led him up the stairs.

When the door was firmly shut and locked, I drew out a small pipe.

"Please," I said, motioning to the floor. "Make yourself comfortable."

Quincy glanced at the long, dark object in my hands. "As you desire," he murmured. Looking at the bed, he said, "Would you not be more comfortable there?"

"We are dealing with fire, and I'd rather not an errant spark ignite and engulf us in flames. I am subject to very few mortal perils, but fire is still one of them."

"I see." He gathered pillows in his arms and placed them along the floor. Soon we were surrounded and had many to prop our backs against.

Taking out a small, embossed silver case, I said to him, "So you are unafraid of death, of danger? Are you willing to take a risk with me?" I opened the silver case to reveal a black, sticky tar-like substance.

His eyes widened. "Yes."

"Even if it means never opening your eyes again? Meeting that dark god, Death?"

"Yes."

He is different, this mortal, I thought. Most shriek and wail against the inevitable call, but he did not even blink at my words.

I dug my fingers into the dark paste.

"Bring that lamp over."

He didn't move.

I cocked my eye at him.

"You know, there is a thing as manners," he said, settling himself deeper into the pillows.

"I could slit your throat right now and not have a moment's regret." I rubbed the paste together until it had formed a small ball.

Still, he settled himself deeper into the pillows.

I huffed. "Please."

Smiling, he obliged. Thinking about doing the same with his eye, I stabbed the pea-sized ball with a needle. I held it over the flame, until it began to burn. After a few moments, it turned a golden color, the same as tangerines, the summer sun: all the things that I had left behind when my sun set forever. When it began to bubble, I stretched it, thick and pliant between two needle points. Quincy was mesmerized.

"Why?" he asked.

"It cooks the opium better, if you stretch it out."

"No, I mean," he stayed my hands for just a moment, and I felt a small thrill rush through my stomach. I told myself it was only the anticipation of smoking. "Why do this thing?" He motioned to the pipe and the sweet essence of poppy.

I resumed my stretching and cooking. "I want to see if you are really as brave as you seem to be."

Liar. Tell him how the little girls made you feel. Tell him how the images of being sold brought forth images buried so deep you forgot how they came to be there in the first place.

"Liar," he echoed my thoughts. "I have played cards with many a gentleman and many a rascal, and I can say for certain, that you, beautiful madam, are lying." He paused, and looked at me, as though studying me, examining me. "You may have even been lying about being a vampire."

Carefully, I set down the opium on the little tray before us. Carefully, I shifted, so that I would not knock over the flame.

Then I pounced.

My hands flew out, grabbing his throat, even as my fangs extended. The impact pressed him against the wall.

"Look at me." I was panting. I wanted to take him right there, but I waited. "Does this look like the face of a liar to you now?"

Finally, fear. Finally, he saw my teeth and saw that I was telling the truth, that I was not a madwoman, that I did not pretend to be anything other than what I was.

I withdrew my hand. The opium was ready.

Rolling it into a small little ball, I placed it carefully in the pipe. Leaning close to the flame of the lamp, I inhaled until the ball caught flame and I could draw in the sweet smoke. The rush of it filled my lungs, went straight to my brain. It made everything around me calm, still, unlike the eternal storm in my mind.

I extended the pipe to Quincy, and he took it without a word. As he inhaled, I knew the delicious poison filled his veins, made his eyelids droop, bade heaven come to him, even as I knew I would drag him to hell.

"Many men have died from this," I said, taking back the pipe. "Why are you not afraid?"

Just as suddenly as I had lunged for him, he lunged for me. His mouth crashed against mine with a ferocity that I did not think this man possessed. The kiss burned against me, scorching me, even more than the smoke had. He tasted of wildflowers, of soot, of sunshine. His lips wrapped me in their velvety embrace, made my insides quiver, even as I told myself it was the effects of the poppy flower.

He withdrew, leaving a searing heat against my lips. I licked them, keeping my eyes firmly on his.

"If I am to die, what better sight than you before my eyes?"

I regarded this man who liked to play with fire.

"Why are you unafraid?"

Quincy ran a hand through his hair.

"How did you come to be a vampire?"

"Tell me, you insufferable human."

"Ladies first."

A growl rumbled low in my throat. "Very well. A story for a story."

As the euphoria began to take hold of us, Quincy reached for me. He might have been curling up with a lion for all he cared. I began to tell him things that I had not told another soul in hundreds of years.

Chapter 19

From the first instant I saw him, I knew that he wanted me. Yet he was the best at concealing his feelings, and that trait never left him in the centuries we were together. His eyes, black as a raven's wing roamed over the slaves at the market, which I was a part of, as if he had no interest in purchasing any today. His hair matched his eyes, although his skin was pale, blanched from staying indoors, free from having to do labor, no doubt. He had a sharp nose, a high forehead, and he towered over everyone else in the crowd. He worse the rich clothes of a wealthy nobleman, and by the looks of his fur cloak, he had gold to pour into the barbarians' greedy hands. Although his glance passed over me quickly, I could feel his attention linger, as if there had been a rope between us, from my navel connected to his.

I pulled my woolen shift tighter across my chest, as the cold wind picked up. Rubbing the coarse wool between my fingers, I relished how bright my clothes still were, with all the different colors that my people wore. We were not afraid to wear bright purple, wild emerald, startling sapphire. Others might hide behind the browns and grays of the mountains, but we always kept enough money in our meager coffers for dyes. If life was not meant to be lived brilliantly, what was the point?

Shivering in the night, I hated standing in the freezing air, as I had done for months now. I had traveled hundreds of miles, always bound at my wrists, and sometimes my ankles, forbidden to move farther than was absolutely necessary. When I had to relieve myself, someone was always required to go with me. When my village was attacked, there had not been enough time to even scream, as the barbarians bound and gagged up, forcing us to be slaves, carrying us to the local markets.

They had taken all of us. My entire family was bound in the same procession, and every night, we clung to each other. The barbarians allowed us that much. My mother and father comforted all of us, their five children, through the long days and nights of servitude. We wept into their arms, and they told us that we would always be together. I clung to that lie as a drowning man clings to a rope pulling him to shore. I believed it with all my beating, bloody heart.

The dark mountains towered behind us, as the torches illuminated our faces. We would normally be sold during the daylight, when the markets had the most people, but the barbarians were anxious to be rid of us and fill their leather satchels with gold as soon as possible.

The man sauntered between the rows of slaves, with an expression of boredom, yet I knew he was keen to buy someone. I did not know his purpose, and I did not know the depths of his evil then, but I knew that whoever dealt in human flesh was someone to be wary of.

Our eyes met, and I shivered, more from his gaze than from the cutting wind. It was almost hypnotic, the look in his eyes. The corners of his mouth tilted up ever so slightly, and he reminded me of a cat who had finally caught his mouse. I wanted to fall into his gaze and run screaming at the same time. I stared back, intent on defying this man who was used to getting his own way.

"And what of her?" he said, his voice a deep, rich baritone. It sounded as htough the mountains themselves were singing, a rich, earthy voice. When Lucifer himself spoke to mortals, I imagined his voice would sound like this man's. He pointed to the woman next to me, a beauty in everything: her face, body, mind, and soul. We had become friends of a sort along the awful, winding trail through the mountains. She was kind and good, and nothing at all like me.

A barbarian, reeking of sweat and stale alcohol immediately jumped forward. "An excellent choice your Excellency," the man groveled. He spoke the language of the land, albeit in a heavily accent voice. He had been over the mountains enough to learn the basics of bartering. Besides, money talks on its own. "She is one of our finer women. Her hands are dainty and still soft, her face could make angels weep, and I assure you, she is most delicious without her clothes." The man, if he could be called such, grinned. He had "tasted" all of us; when I had tried to fight back, he had punched me hard in the stomach.

"I see," said the man, looking straight at me. My stomach fluttered. "And how much is she?"

I instantly knew that my friend would not leave with this man. Perhaps that was for the best, after all. I am not sure she could have born the years and not come out broken on the other side of the millennia.

The barbarian was all but rubbing his hands together, his slanted eyes sparkling with greed. "Your excellency has the most refined of tastes. I will let her go for a trifle," he said. "Ten pounds of gold."

"You must be mad, my friend," said the man, turning to the barbarian. "She is special, and no doubt beautiful, but I cannot give away ten pounds of gold for one slave. The price is far too high." Again he looked at me, but this time he smiled. "Three pounds."

"Your most kind and worthy excellency, you do me pain!" the barbarian wailed. I rolled my eyes at the dramatics of the market. "I could never release such a beautiful and exceptional creature for the pitiful sum of three pounds.

Just get it over with, I thought. The night was dark, not even a sliver of moon to illuminate the land, and my toes were becoming numb in my thin, leather shoes.

He walked over and stood in front of her, but I could feel his eyes slowly glide to me. I felt a heat and my nipples tightened beneath my shift. He was handsome, there was no denying it. He had all the grace and power of a wolf. I eyed the breadth of his shoulders and my breath hitched.

He lifted a hand and gently cupped her chin, and I swear I could feel that hand on me. When he lifted his fingers to tuck a strand of hair behind her ear, it was my own that tingled with delight. Against all rationality, I became jealous of the attention he was giving her. I both loved and loathed him in that instant.

"Five pounds, and not a penny more," he said. My heart was beating in my chest to have him so near.

The barbarian shifted his eyes, torn between a quick profit now or waiting to fetch a larger sum at the bigger, city markets in the coming days. In truth, he could have sold the woman for twenty, but money in the pocket is always better than speculation of tomorrow.

"Your excellency...I don't...I am not sure," he babbled. No wonder they were called barbarians; their speech resembled nothing than gibberish.

"What about her?" the man said, turning to me. My world slowed. His black eyes filled my entire sight, and they seemed to hold me in their power.

"I leave with my family, or not at all," I said, thrusting my chin up. I looked to them, scattered through the lines, and my mother was weeping, a change from what usually occurred. There were so many nights where I had been afraid of this very moment, but now that it had come, I was ready to fight like a mountain lion.

The barbarian wrenched my ear and shouted, "Only speak when you are spoken to!" He screamed loud enough to wake the dead. Turning to the man, he said, "My apologies, your excellency. As you can see, we have had difficulties with that one. She is not even fit to clean the horse shit from your boots."

The man lifted an eyebrow. "Indeed? How much?" he asked.

"I cannot get rid of her, even for a half penny, but my leader will throttle me if I do not ask for at least one pound," said the barbarian. "Please, your excellency, you would do far better with your first choice."

"Done. One pound," said the man, pulling a gold piece from a small leather bag.

The barbarian looked astonished.

"Untie her, and be quick about it," said the man. "The moonlight is waning." He smiled, and it seemed as though there were some kind of joke about that.

When the barbarian cut the ropes around my wrists, the ones that had chaffed and turned them red and raw through the weeks, I began to scream. I ran to my mother and father, clinging to them, holding them as tightly as I could. My siblings too, were all wailing, and I was not going to go with that dark, terrible, and beautiful man.

"I tried to warn you, your excellency," muttered the barbarian, glad to have been rid of me. He would drink well tonight. "But now as she is your problem, I must attend to other clients." He stalked off.

The man picked me up as if I weighed no more than a feather. His iron grip pulled my hands from my mother's, and he threw me over his shoulder. He gripped my thighs, and it felt like a sweet breaking of all the bonds I knew and held dear. I kicked and screamed, hitting him, failing with all my power. Punching him felt like beating at a wall. His flesh did not give, and he did not appear to suffer pain. That should have been my first clue. I should have thrown myself from the mountain cliffs right then, but I was still under the delusional hope that I would somehow make it back to my parents.

He had come in a carriage, and four huge, black horses were tied to the back. He opened the door, oblivious to my screams, and the stares of the entire market and threw me inside. I landed on the softest pillows and warmest blankets. Already my body welcomed leaving the frigid wind.

Slaves usually protested against their own purchase, but none cried out as loud as I did. No one wanted to remain with her family as much as I. We were a wandering people, and some thought of us as rootless. Far from it. We had our history, our roots, our lives buried so deep in the rich, black soil of the mountains that we always knew where home was. It was not tied to the land but each other. As long as we had our families, we were neither homeless nor destitute.

Yet now I was an orphan.

I turned to him and spat. Instead of slapping me, as would any other man of that era, he grabbed me by the chin and kissed me. My senses were instantly flooded with the scent of him, the smell of pine and burning wood, of musk, and the sickly sweet aroma of dying flowers. Against my wishes, my lips responded to his, forming to his, moving with the energy he gave. My head swam, and before I passed out, he lifted his face from mine but stayed a mere hair's breadth away.

"Do not try to jump out, or you will die. Do not try to run, or you will die. If you ever leave my side, you will die," he warned.

"Is that a promise?" I said, wiping away his taste with the back of my hand.

He laughed. "I am very glad I chose you," he said. "We will have so much fun."

"I want my family," I said.

"I am your family now," he responded, and closed the door, locking it.

Chapter 20

I tried to run.

Of course I tried to run. My family had just been ripped from me, I had seen a man without a reflection in a mirror, and my utter disregard for prudence pushed me to flee in the dead of night. I could not have known that night was the worst time to leave.

It was time to confront what was right before me: there was something deeply wrong with Victor. He looked like a human, had the shape and appearance of one, but something deep in my gut told me he was not. I did not know whether to think he was a demon from the Christian religion, or something far scarier from my own tribe's tales. We told stories of awful creatures who could turn into wolves, if they were the seventh son of the seventh son, or of beings who drank blood and could only be killed with iron.

Whatever he was, I feared him, and knew I had to escape. It did not matter if his face looked like that of the statue of Gabriel in the village church, or that his body was lithe like a panther's. My life was not worth his smooth voice, nor his hypnotic stare. All urges to stay fled when I thought to the moment of the mirror.

I lay in my bed, the smooth cotton sheets almost to my chin. My heart pounded. I lay still, trying to listen to the sound of the castle, to see if he were still awake. I could detect nothing, no footstep, no door being shut. The night was as still as the castle; the wind did not blow against the windows and howl, as it had for so many nights, nor did the bats shriek in the night. The silence was almost as eerie as the noises of the night.

Carefully, I raised myself from the bed and quickly tied up my boots, the strong, sturdy ones Victor had given me. I already had on my cloak, and my pack was ready by my door. I stole quietly through the castle, alert for the slightest sound or indication that Victor was following me. I felt like a mouse, reacting to the slightest shadow, terrified of seeing the shape of the cat.

Escaping through the kitchen door, I fled into the velvet darkness of the night. My only plan was to race to the village as quickly as I could, to find some shelter with the first family I could find, then quickly make my way westward, to follow the slave train heading in that direction.

The night was cold, although clear, and the moon shone brightly down, full as a pregnant woman's belly. The pine trees thrust up from the earth like spears, and their scent blew toward me on the breeze. I pulled my hood over my head and tied my cloak tighter. Sticks and leaves crunched under my feet, their earthy scent mixing with that of the pine. I heard a lone owl hooting, and I wondered if the predator would catch his prey tonight.

I ran down the mountain, my cloak streaming behind me as I did. My only thought was to enter the first house that let me. I heard a wolf howl in the distance, and I ran faster. The village was some five miles away, and I had to take short breaks to catch my breath, but I still pressed on, the thought of putting as much distance between myself and Victor as possible driving me forward. The wind blew toward me, and I thought I heard laughing in the distance.

What if I never find my family again? I thought. Then I pushed that thought to the side. I could not dwell on such dismal notions; otherwise, I might never make it down the mountain.

The village was small, with timber houses and thatched roofs. Only a few lights were burning in the windows at this hour, just enough to give me hope. I stepped up to a door and pounded. My blood sang in my ears, from running and from the trepidation of being discovered by

Victor, and I strained to hear any sort of response from inside. None. I tried the next door but received the same response. Going from door to door, I pounded, pleaded for Christian sanctuary against a fiend.

Finally, someone opened a slit in their front door, just enough to where I could see only their eyes.

"Go away, girl," said a gruff, female voice. "Do not bring that monster down here."

"Please," I begged. "Give me shelter for just one night, and I will leave before daybreak."

The old woman shook her head, her grizzled, gray hair frizzy and wild with each shake. "No," she said fiercely. "Even if we did not already know of the horrors of that...man, I could not let a filthy heathen into my house."

The refusal to enter hit me worse than the insult; it was like a blow to the stomach.

"Please, tell me," I begged again. "What do you mean? What horrors?"

But all the woman did was scream, "Go away!" and slammed the little slit shut. I could hear her locking the door bolts from the inside.

I continued to pound on her door, shouting and begging for refuge.

The moonlight was shining just bright enough that I could see a shadow fall across the door.

I turned around and Victor grabbed me.

"Little sneak," he murmured with affection against my ear. He lifted me as easily as one could lift a child and carried me all the way back to the castle. We moved so quickly that the we seemed to float over the ground. He pressed me so close to him that once more I could smell his intoxicating aroma, and to my shame, I became aroused. His arms felt like iron bars beneath me, and I wondered how strong he truly was.

When we entered the castle, he did not stop at the door. No, he carried me all the way up the stairs, up to the highest tower and dropped me onto the bed.

His face seemed to be in a terrifying rage and delight at the same time. As he put me down, I noticed his hands shook.

"It is earlier than I expected, but all the same, very good," he said.

My body sank into the sheets and pillows. He looked so dangerous standing in the moonlight.

"Oh my dear, I told you that if you ever tried to run, I would kill you," he said.

I swallowed, my heart in my throat. "What do you mean?" I whispered. "Are you going to kill me?"

"Yes," he responded instantly. "But you will live."

He smiled, and I saw his glistening, white fangs emerge from his gums. He took a step and moved so fast that he was instantly by my side. Grasping my face in his hands, he began to kiss me.

I longed for his body, longed for the love that I thought he could fulfill in me. I knew he was a monster, but still I fell into his passionate embrace with abandon, because he had hypnotized me so. When he looked at me, it was like I was the only thing that mattered in the whole world. His fiery jealousy inflamed some egoistic part of me that wanted to be loved so ardently that I was willing to risk danger with a madman.

Wrapping my arms around him, I removed his outer coat while he undid the laces of my dress. He ripped it off and threw it to the ground, revealing my under-shift. He pulled it over my head and suddenly, I was naked and vulnerable. I needed to see his chest, needed to feel his smooth skin under my fingertips, so I removed his shirt, pulling it over his head. All the while, we kissed and touched each other, and I was so angry with him that I wanted to hurt him while I could. I grasped a handful of his hair and yanked back, and he inhaled sharply. I bit his collarbone so hard that I drew little droplets of blood from his skin.

By chance, some entered into my mouth, and they were so sweet, and so heavenly that I began to lap at his skin with my tongue. As perplexed as I felt at how blood could taste so rich, still, I did not stop.

He returned my favor and yanked my head back, and whispered into my ear, "All in good time," and he positioned himself on top of me.

I was ready. My body ached for his, and I took him in my hand and guided him inside me. From terror or pleasure I still do not know, but my body was as willing and supple as any woman's on her wedding night.

When he entered me, I gave out a little cry. It was as though he touched something deep inside that I scarce knew existed. He began to rock back and forth and my pleasure grew.

Some part of my mind screamed that this was wrong, that he would kill me, but I silenced it with all the strength remaining to me. That furious part of me ran my nails down his back, imparting both pain and pleasure to us both. All I could see was his eyes in front of me; all I could feel were his strong fingers playing my body like a fiddle.

My excitement, and his built.

Just as I was at the pinnacle of pleasure, when I felt that my world would shatter, it did. He opened his mouth and bit down on my neck. I cried out in pleasure, for he had pierced me again. As my body shuddered, releasing into the climax of our moment, my heart pumped harder than it ever had before. All th sweetness of the feeling seeped into me, and every pull of blood that he took from me only heightened the feeling.

My body soon fell in the languorous state after lovemaking, but something was wrong. I was becoming too lethargic, too at ease. I realized that he had not released me from his grip. All my energy was vanishing, and I did not know when or if he would stop. I lifted my fist to pound against his back, but I was already so weak that it made no difference. He continued to drink my lifeforce, and I cursed myself for letting him have it.

Every sensation became sharper, as it never had before. The feel of the silky sheets under me, the smell of the night orchids in the air, and the howl of the wolves outside all seemed heightened, bigger, clearer.

At once, he released me, two drops of blood dripping down his mouth. He licked them away as if a cat might. My body swam in a pool of ecstasy and misery. I was so anemic that I could not lift my head from the pillows, and darkness pressed at the corners of my vision. I knew I was about to die. Feeling like a huge failure that I did not go to my family, I tried to rise even then from my position, only to hear him laugh.

"You still fight, do you? Admirable as that is, I know you cannot," he said. "Just let it take hold of you. It is inevitable."

"Nothing is inevitable," I whispered. "Except that I will kill you."

He chuckled, arrogant, gloating. My vision dimmed, and I saw visions of heaven and hell. Victor bit into his wrist and held his dripping wound over my face.

Blood trickled into my open mouth, and if it had been sweet before, it was like honey now, thick and rich. Some instinct made me grab hold of his wrist, clamping down, drawing blood into me like I had drawn his body into mine. The world spun around me, and with each pull, I became stronger, losing whatever weakness that had held me down before.

Whenever I felt at the height of it, I experienced a greater release than our union before. Indeed, it was the release of the very shackles of death had over me until that point. Discharging that weight, that horrendous, heavy burden was the purest form of bliss I had ever known.

My eyes snapped open. I looked into Victor now with blood-red eyes. My strength was immense, my senses were heightened, emotions more so, and everything seemed ten times greater than it had in life. I no longer felt the unending dread of death stalking me at every turn.

My hatred and love for Victor magnified a hundredfold. And I knew that I had become damned, a legend, a prowler of the night.

I had become a vampire.

Chapter 21

He was such a beautiful liar. He was an expert, really, because he told me a blend of truths and fiction. In my newborn state, I could have believed everything, and I did.

I remember my hands looked like they had been formed from marble. They were smooth, ethereal. When I looked at them, I could see the ridges of my fingerprints: even further, I could see the tiny ridges inside the ridges that formed the canyons. Each part seemed llinking to the next, like a great jigsaw puzzle.

When I looked around the room, everything seemed brighter, although it was night. The moonlight shining through the window was like an ocean of ligt, bathing everything in a pearlescent glow. Looking at Victor, I saw that he was smirking.

"now I have a companion," he said softly.

I jerked my head up, horror and fascination filling me. "What have you done?" I whispered. I leaped off the bed, moving faster than I ever had as a human. With each moment, it felt like I had barely thought before my body responded. I pulled my dress over my head, temporarily embarrassed and vulnerable to be seen in such a state.

Something caused me to stop. With all my keen sense, I could hear things that I never noticed before as a human: the wind flowing through the tiny cracks in the castle, creating soft, ghostly wails; the crunch of grass outside, as thousands of insects and mice moved through the fields; even the sppech of the villagers, some five miles away, I could hear if I concentrated hard enough.

It was what I did not hear that horrified me.

My heart.

I put my hand to my chest.

Nothing.

I screamed, wondering what monster I had become. I flew at Victor, hands outstretched into claws, and this time, I knew that I could hurt him.

"What did you do to me?" I said, pounding my fists at his chest. He blocked me, and tired to throw me off, but I was so much more powerful now, and I did not bend easily to him. I kicked at him, trying to land a blow wherever I could.

"I gave you a home," he said, still smirking, which only enraged me further.

"I had a home!" I screamed. "Take me back!"

"Listen," he commanded, pulling my arms back. He pinned me to the bed, hovering over me. Something in his voice made me pay attention, forced me to calm. "You can never go back. This is your new life now, and you should be happy you have it. You are free from aging, free from death! You will never become bent nor broken, stooped with the crushing weight of years. You will never know disease, nor pain and humiliation that comes from old age. You will retain all your youthful beauty forever."

My anger burned against him like it never had before. "Did I ask for this?" I shouted.

"Yes," he responded viciously. "You did when you fled down the mountain. You did not listen, and I told you what would happen if you disobeyed me."

I freed my arms from his grasp, something impossible had I been human, and managed to punch him in the stomach. He bent, toppled toward the bed, and I tried to run for the door.

In a flash, he was before me. He inhaled shakily, and said, "I knew that I chose well when I picked you. You are truly a remarkable creature."

"What must I do?" I demanded. "If there is one thing that I learned as a slave it is that nothing in this world comes free. What damnation must I live with to earn this eternal life?"

He looked at me for a moment, assessing my as though I were an insect on a board. "Such intellect," he murmured. "Come with me."

He did not take me, but merely walked toward the window. I felt myself drawn to him like iron drawn to iron. He stepped out onto the ledge and grasped the jutting bricks of the castle wall.

He found the tiniest cracks in the walls and managed to cling to the bricks. "Come," he commanded and stepped out.

I stepped up to the ledge. My stomach flipped around when I saw the drop of hundreds of feet below. Dizzy with the height, I had an old human fear of falling to my death.

"You will not fall," he said. "Follow me."

Again, I felt that irresistible pull to him, as though I could not say now. I stepped out onto the ledge and followed him. The window blew strongly at this height, and I imagined it would blow me right off, shattering my bones below.

But my fingers dug into the cracks; I could feel the grind of the stones under my skin, and with my newfound strength, I could climb the wall find the slightest crack and crevice to hold onto as I ascended.

When he reached the roof, Victor gave a great push with his arms, and hoisted himself up. I did the same, marveling at how easy it all was. My body felt lighter than a leaf tossed by the wind.

The stars burned cold and bright above us. I could see them twinkling, and with my new vision, I saw that they were not all the same color, as I had previously thought as a human. They were not simply white or cream. Some burned blue, others red. Still others ,far off, shone the faintest purple. I marveled at how they winked and flickered, and I soon lost my anger with Vicotr for a moment. As a newborn, it was so easy to get lost in every new sensation.

"Look out, and tell me what you see," said Vicotr motioning with his hands.

I saw endless miles of dark, green forest, the jagged mountains in the distance scraping at the sky, the faint flickering of village torchlights. A river sparkled nearby, and I knew that it led to a crystal clear lake.

"Wild country," I replied. "A place teeming with savage beauty."

"This is now your home," he replied. "You are tied to the earth. You cannot leave here or else you will perish the Final and Ultimate Death."

The blow hit me harder than the horror of what I was. I needed to roam; it had been in my family's blood for generations. Always, we had wandered from one place to another, never being satisfied with staying in one location for very long. There was so much to see in the world, so many fantastic sights and breath-taking wonders. I could not imagine staying in one place.

"Why?" I whispered. Even in the moonlight, with his smirk, Victor was handsome beyond all reasoning.

He shrugged. "I did not make the rules of existence. All I know is that our blood and the magic that drives it is tied to the earth. Once we leave this wild country, we will turn to dust," he said.

I paused, letting his horrible words settle over me.

"What else?" I demanded. "What other limitations are there?"

For once, his smirk left his face. "There are mainly two, and they are as inflexible as hardened steel. One: that you cannot survive outside when the sun is up. You must be deeply concealed, so no ray falls on you. If not, you will turn to ash and blow away."

Even then, I thought about waiting on the roof until the sun came up. I could simply let its flight fill me and give up this awful change. If I were never to see my family again, onr leave this miserable, harsh land, what was the point?

Victor seemed to guess my thoughts. "You will not stay up here," he said. "A deep need will come over you to hide. It is instinctual, and you cannot fight it."

"Do we" (and how I hated now to use the word "we") have any other fallibilities?" I asked.

How can I one day kill you? I thought.

He still looked grave. "Fire," he said softly. "Our bodies are susceptible to fire. If you cut off a limb, it will either grow back or if you replace it quickly enough, it will join once more with the flesh. If you are stabbed, you will feel pain, but your organs no longer live so that they cannot die."

I nodded. So we could in fact die, but anything sort of fire would not harm us.

Well, they will hurt, but I will not die, I thought.

"And the other?" I prompted. "What must I do to maintain this immortal soul?" I had a feeling it would be worse than the first.

His smile slowly returned, and I felt my stomach clench in fear. "That is the entertaining bit," he said. "You must fulfill yourself with human blood. Nothing else will do. You can try to drink the blood of animals, but eventually, you will fade. If you do not, your body will become a husk, but still you will not die. You will simply live your days in agony, as your veins scream out for the nourishment it needs."

I remembered the draughts of blood I had taken from him during my transformation. Even now, I felt a powerful thirst lurking in the back of my throat. It burned and my vision went red. I felt a pounding in my head, a demand for blood that did not feel evil and so terrified me more.

"You have damned me to this, and I hate you for it," I said.

He laughed, and I wanted to rake my nails down his face. "You will thank me before fifty years have passed. When everyone you know shrivels and finally dies, then you will worship at my feet," he said. He gestured around to the village. "The boundaries of your hunting ground are Transylvania. The mountains to the north and the forest to the west. Do not go beyond these, or else you will surely die." He turned to me and shrugged his left shoulder, as if he had not a care of what I did after that. "Anyone in the villages is fair fame. Children are especially delicious, as their blood is not tainted with age and suffering yet."

Disgusted, I turned away. I was not afraid of blood. Everyone in my family had known how to hunt, as we were travelers and needed fresh meat on our journeys. But this? To hunt my fellow humans?

"They are not your fellows any more than you are human now," Victor said, reading my mind.

His words were colder than the wind. I knew that they were true. I wanted to cry, but my tears felt frozen inside of me.

I looked down at my hands once more, amazed and reveling in their transformation.

"Can I do this?" I whispered. "Can I create another one of us? Another...vampire?" The word felt strange and foreign on my tongue. My humanity clung to itself, even as it seeped out of me. It did not want to be transformed.

Victor shook his head. "Only I have the power to create another," he said. "But your talents and gifts will emerge with time. You have only the years to make you stronger."

He turned and left, flitting from one tower to the next, in huge, leaping bounds. I stayed on the roof until dawn peaked over the edge of the horizon.

When the rays of the sun leached over the earth, he was right: I was unable to fight the instinct to bury myself deep in darkness.

This was to be my home now. I could barely fathom how I would learn to live with this unbearable curse, shouldering it as I had shouldered my fate as a slave. In that instant, all hope of seeing my family again vanished.

He was right about so many things. I did learn. It was surprising how quickly I shed my old humanity, as easily as a snake sheds its skin. I prowled the villages at night, stalked my victims with ease, and relished the thrill of the hunt. Their blood tasted hot and sweet in my mouth, although never as sweet as that first taste. And to my guilt, Victor was right. I soon looked at the old humans with disgust, triumphing that I had beaten death. And after one hundred years, I mourned my original family, as I knew that no one could have survived that long.

As the years passed, Victor became my world. I have never let go of my anger of him, but instead embrace it, fueling my passion for him. I will never forget how he taught me how to hunt, how to be a vampire. Through the years, he gathered my other sisters, and we became a family of sorts. I thought I had everything that I wanted: a family. Victor was my rock, my lust, my reason for living under the moon.

And then Jonathan arrived and shattered my illusion.

Chapter 22

The moon had raced halfway across the sky when I was finished. Somewhere in the course of my ramblings and half-forgotten memories, I had found my way into Quincy's arms. We still lay on the floor, half-propped up by cushions, our heads lounging against one another. With a touch as soft as silk, Quincy was slowly stroking my arm languidly. Finally, he spoke.

"So you were not joking when you said you had come to kill someone," he said.

"Indeed not."

The flame of the lamp flickered in the breeze that gently swept through the room. Our bones were filled with soft magic, radiant warmth. He had survived, this human.

But I do not think that I would let him die.

The thought was mildly surprising.

"You sound trapped."

"I am not."

"Of course, you are. You left the castle, but you are held prisoner in your own mind. It sounds as though you still love this Victor." Up and down, up and down, his fingers creating an oozing electricity along my spine.

"What's love got to do with it? I need him. I hate him. I cannot live without him."

His fingers worked their way up my arm, along my shoulder, and to my neck. In their wake, he left a trail of gooseflesh.

"Sounds like love to me. The worst and best of all passions, mixed."

"He must die."

"Definitely love."

Did he know that he was filling my belly with fire? Did he know that my breasts were swelling, aching to be touched? Still, I balked at his talk of love.

"And what of you?" I asked. "What of your doomed romance? Do you still pine for your—what was her name?"

"Lucy."

"Lucy...her name is a delight." I said these words even as the acid of jealous coated my tongue. "How fairs your lady?"

Quincy sighed softly. "To be honest, not well. I saw her the other day. She looked pallid and weak. Her friend Mina told me that she was been suffering from sleepwalking, and—" he gulped. "Saying the strangest things. Visions. She says she sees a dark man coming to her, visiting her at night."

"Do you miss her?" Why, why did I persist in this sordid fascination to inquire after this woman's health? Even when my stomach revolted against the thought of Quincy thinking about another.

Quincy was quiet for a moment.

"Lucy was everything I thought I wanted—a nice girl of gentle upbringing, a solid step in society. Marriage to her would have raised me from the ranks of a soldier to a more gentlemanly heights. My family still has the stain of coming from humble merchants. But no." His fingers moved to my collarbone. "I now know that I want something outside the normal trapping so f English society. Rather than be confined to a lifetime of dullness and boredom, I want someone more..." Now his wicked fingers were tracing the edge of my hem, along the swell of my breasts. "Dangerous."

"And what will you do when you find this dangerous person?" I asked. I turned so that I could look him in the eyes. "Will you keep her in a cage, a hunting prize, a rug on your floor? Or perhaps stuffed and taxidermied, with marble eyes, a trophy to add to your collection?"

"Of course not; something dangerous needs to roam free."

Roam. Just like his eyes were doing down my chest. They roved even further traveling along every inch of me, and I felt my hackles raise along the back of my neck.

I leaned toward him. "So what is it that you want?" I whispered. Our lips were but a hair's breadth apart.

"Only you."

And then, they touched. I felt that same fire as before, only slower, more excruciating, as it traveled from my lips down my throat and into my stomach. Further, dropping into my belly and spreading to all of my limbs, from the tips of fingers to every last toe. My whole body ached with longing to be held by him.

It was then that something broke inside me. Perhaps it was the sweetness of Quincy's touch, or the longing in his fingers, or even the slow pull of the poppy, but a wellspring of emotion poured forth.

I had told Quincy everything there was to know about me, and he did not run, not as so many humans would do. He knew my faults, could see the evil that lived inside me, and wanted me all the same. Perhaps the biggest thing, the thing that made me care about him the most was that he had not thus far tried to control me. He wanted a lion but did not want to tame her.

Quincy pulled back when he felt the wetness upon my cheeks.

"What's wrong?" he whispered. "What did I do?"

Where did these tears come from? How did Quincy melt this glacier of a heart long enough for there to be water leaking out?

"Nothing." I swiped at my eyes. I pulled him back to me. "Take me."

No other prompting was needed.

Quincy reached around and pulled the strings and laces of my dress, our interrupted dalliance coming to its completion. He pulled my dress down, and my nipples tightened in the cool night air.

He gazed at me, his eyes still glazed, smoke and heat and desire. He bent his head to me and murmured, "They're beautiful," and he took one quivering tip in his mouth.

My back arched against my will. There was fire and there was electricity, but Quincy's tongue brought power to the fore. With each kiss, his tongue lapped against me, as delicate as a kitten's, even as his hand cupped my other breast. He kneaded it in his expert fingers.

"When did Englishmen become such good lovers?" I whispered.

"One learns a trick or two," he murmured, switching sides.

When he gently bit down, I cried out, loving the growing throbbing in my groin.

Slowly, he peeled my dress from me, and as my skin was exposed to the night, it became covered in gooseflesh, raised, every nerve standing at attention. I suddenly wanted this man deep inside me, needed to bring him to the same level of pleasure as I experienced.

I suddenly straightened and pinned him down. I did not bother with the buttons, ripping his shirt down the front, exposing his hard chest and rippled abs he must have gained whilst in the military. Pulling off his shirt, I threw it across the room, eager to liberate him from his other garments. My fingers were swift and deft as I worked at his pants.

Tugging them off, all that was left were Quincy's undershorts. My mouth grew dry at the sight of his manhood pressing against them, leaving a small, wet stain on the front. I ripped his undershorts, springing his glorious member free.

"My lady, those were custom-made," he said, looking at the heap of now tattered clothes on the floor. His tone was that of shock but his eyes gleamed playful.

"No apologies," I said and bent to take him in my mouth.

This time, it was Quincy who arched, and I loved seeing the look of ecstasy cross his face. He tasted salty, delicious, and as my mouth moved down the length of him, he became even harder as I stroked.

"Enough," he growled. "Come to me."

Still I lashed him with my tongue.

"Not yet," I murmured. He pulsed against my tongue.

"Please." The word barely escaped his lips.

How could I withstand that pristine sense of English etiquette? I obliged him.

Positioning myself on top of him, I sank down, our mutual groans mingling together. His flesh fit perfectly into mine. He was neither too small nor too extravagant, the length suiting my deepest needs. He touched that center point of pleasure and I cried out. I began rocking my hips in our delicious dance.

He grabbed my hips with his hands, and we found our rhythm. With each breath, the pressure built, stirring us. I looked into his eyes, and I wanted to control him, dominate him. I needed to hear him, needed to hear his sighs and cries. I began to rock faster.

"God," he said. He groaned, looking at me with a mixture of awe and carnality.

His sigh of gratification inflamed me even more. I loved being the one who made that look cross his face, who made his brows come together in an expression that seemed to be pain but betrayed deep satisfaction.

"He's not here right now," I said, and I rode him harder.

This human was reaching his limit. I could feel him growing stiffer inside me. Because I knew that he was growing closer to the pinnacle, so was I.

Suddenly, I stopped.

Quincy's eyes snapped open. His hands gripped me harder. "Don't stop!"

He pulsed deep inside me, and I relished being the one who dictated how often the indulgence was dealt.

I rocked forward once. Twice.

"Please."

Then he looked up at me, and I swear I saw something in his eyes. It was not love. It was not desire. It was something that I had not seen before in five hundred years. It might have been respect.

It was then that I lost control. The heat concentrated inside me and suddenly released. As the throbbing took me over in waves of deep, dizzying bliss, I cried out and ground my hips against his, faster and faster.

Quincy groaned and gripped my legs, and I knew that he had reached his own pleasure. He pounded his hips against mine, and we lost ourselves in ecstasy.

Chapter 23

We lied there on the floor, spent and heaving, our chests rising and falling like waves in an ocean. The thunderous echoes of my climax still rippled through me. I felt slated, easing into a dreamy, comforting trance.

Quincy drew a powerful arm around me, holding me tightly. I let him. For once, I did not want to run away. He laced his fingers around mine.

"You held back," he murmured against my ear.

"Yes." The last remaining effects of the opium were draining away, even as a deeper pleasure came to replace it.

"Why?"

I spoke to the still-lit lamp in front of us. "Because I did not want to hurt you. I took you as a mortal would."

Quincy remained silent, although I could feel the question hovering on his lips. Then: "Would you kill me? Do you have an uncontrollable desire to drink my blood?"

I snorted. "Don't be daft. This is an English expression I love. Yes, the urge to drink from you is always there, but after five hundred years of being a vampire, I have at least a little self-control."

Quincy's mouth quirked up into a smile.

"I do not want to harm you by force of lovemaking. If I gave you every ounce of power I have, your heart would not be able to bear it."

"I see." The flame flicked and danced before us. "But that is a risk that I am willing to take."

We sighed in unison, lounging in the sweet aftershocks of our lovemaking.

But suddenly, I sat up. I needed to roam. I was filled with a kind of energy that I had not had in so long. After being shackled to Victor's castle for so long, I yearned to see the world, beginning with London. I turned to Quincy.

"Come," I said, tossing aside the pillows and blowing out the lamps. "Much moonlight remains."

Standing up, I tugged on my dress and tied the strings. Quincy looked at the heap of clothes on the floor.

"The buttons don't matter," I said brusquely. "Neither your undergarments."

Quincy only cocked an eyebrow up, a grin spreading across his face.

Some minutes later, we were strolling arm and arm down the streets of London. We made our way out of the slums where thieves prowled and prostitutes called and entered into the finer districts, where trees were guarded with gates, flowers bloomed along the sidewalks, and gardens sprawled in cultivated splendor. The air changed from dense, heavy smog to perfumes of lilies and chrysanthemums.

We came upon a huge, white building, that stretched into the distance. Grecian-style columns towered over us, and an arched entrance read, "London Zoo."

"Zoo. What is it?" I asked.

"A place where wild animals are kept."

"And they roam where they wished?"

Quincy chuckled softly. "Hardly. They are kept in cages."

"Sounds intriguing. Let us enter."

Quincy looked at the locked and barred entrance. "I believe it is closed for the night."

"Oh you of little imagination."

Wrapping one hand Quincy's waist, I held him tightly as I pushed with all my strength and jumped. We sailed through the air, landing on the top of the wall. From there, we walked along the parapet until we came upon a tree situated against the wall and climbed down.

The ripe stench of animal sweat hung in the air. Faint growls stirred in the distance.

Quincy was right. Animals of all sorts were kept in circular cages, the bars as thick as my arm. I saw animals that I had only seen in pictures in books: fierce eagles, cunning serpents, and chittering monkeys who screamed when we came close. There was an Arabian camel with two humps that spat at us when we refused to give it food. We strolled, down the alleys, my eyes drinking in the sights of beasts I had never thought I would see. African hippos slept in the water, their tiny little ears twitching against flies. A monstrous beast Quincy called an elephant dipped its enormous nose in my direction. It looked clumsy, but with delicate elegance, it picked up a stick off the ground and extended it to me in an offer of friendship.

All of it was a wonder to behold. Yet, when I spied the lions and tigers in their cages, I shook in silent fury. The tiger's eyes shone like marbles in the moonlight. It was awake, not walking, but simply lounging, its enormous paws dangling out of the cage. Its eyes held a sadness I understood all too well.

I turned to Quincy. "Why are they locked up?"

Quincy regarded the enormous paws of the tiger. "I suppose so that people can look at them without fear of getting mauled."

I sucked in the air through my teeth. "And what of its life? Does it have nothing better to do than sit around, being looked at? It needs to hunt, to kill. To move about where it wishes."

"Ow, ow, ow!"

"Sorry," I said, releasing Quincy's hand. I had been squeezing it until the bones grinded together. I held the tiger's gaze with my own. I swear I could see its soul.

"Why keep something so beautiful and deadly locked up?"

I turned to Quincy for confirmation, but he was not looking at the tiger. He was looking at me.

"I think a better question is, why would something so beautiful and deadly keep herself locked in a cage?"

He moved on.

After a moment of silence, so did I.

"That was not the first moment that I have seen a lion," he said.

The night air smelled of jasmine, despite the ripe scent of animal fur and sweat. I inhaled easily and turned my face toward my lover.

"No?"

He shook his head. "I once stared a beautiful huntress in the eye. She was the terror of the night and no one could best her."

"Go on."

"I was stationed in Cape Town, at nearly the edge of the earth. We were so far south in Africa that it even became chilly in winter. The golden desert sands turned into lush African brush. My regiment was there, ostensibly for king and country, but we all knew that the real reason was diamonds. We were to take the position from the Boers, by any means necessary."

"A military man," I reflected. "That is why you are so..."

Quincy cocked an eyebrow.

"...strict."

"I'm strict?" Quincy laughed. "I thought my days of following orders were behind me."

"You walk as though your life depends on your spine being as straight as possible, and you have a way of being tidy in all things," I responded, remembering the way Quincy had delicately placed the pipe on the little tray, just so.

"Anyway, in between skirmishes with the damned Dutch descendants, and avoiding getting our heads blown off, Africa provided the most beautiful sites and the most terrible game to hunt." His white teeth flashed in the dark. "The most exciting thing that you ever experienced."

We turned a corner and listened to the monkeys chittering wildly.

"Rolling green hills, snow-capped mountains, jagged cliffs; all of it served to hide enormous beasts: leopards, rhinoceros, buffalo, elephants, and the most cunning of all: lions."

My mouth went dry at the thought of the open space. I knew what he was remembering: the uptick in heartbeat as he approached his prey; the smell of the wind blowing through the dry grasses, the feel of sweat trickling down his brow.

Quincy laughed softly. "But there was one lion that was the most fearsome, the smartest," he continued. "No one knew why she attacked villages. She did not look starving, nor was the season any worse than normal. There was no drought nor want of food. Still, night after night, she would prowl into the local village and steal away a child or drunken man, too foolish to realize that he shouldn't go out after dark."

"So my men and I decided that we'd had enough of fighting for diamonds that we'd never see, and tired of seeing men's hands get chopped off for them, so we began to hunt her."

A spark lit up Quincy's face, one that I had not seen before.

"For seven days and seven nights, we tracked her. We hardly ate. We barely slept. Our senses became so keen that we could hear the snap of a twig two hundred meters off. I could smell anything that came close."

Quincy then leaned in close. "And finally, we learned her trick. There was not one lionness, but two. One would distract the hunters, while the other made the kill."

I swallowed. Adrenaline was pounding through Quincy's blood, giving it a heady aroma. I inhaled, my mouth watering. Slowly, my fangs extended.

"We had spotted the other lion. We were sneaking up on her, about seven meters away. The grasses, pale yellow and razor sharp pricked beneath us. We cocked our guns. All I could think about was breathing, about the gentle, steady flow of air in my lungs." Quincy swallowed. "And then I heard the bushes rustle."

I knew this moment, savored it with him. To have an opponent to be your equal.

"I whipped my head around. There, barely two meters away, was the main lioness. Her huge, golden eyes filled my vision. In that moment, I did not fear death. I thought, if I am to die, then it will be at the hands of a worthy adversary. A master huntress."

When he looked at me then, I swear my heart beat.

"She sprang. I fired."

And I shivered.

Quincy took a deep breath. "After that, the others wanted to bring her back, as you say, a trophy. But I buried her. I could not let something so beautiful, intelligent, and deadly be treated as a toy for us. It pricked at my pride a bit, I admit, but in the end, she needed to be acknowledged. She was my most worthy challenge..."

He took my hand and brought it to his lips. "...until now."

After that, we wandered the grounds of the zoo, until Quincy's jaw nearly cracked from yawning.

"Let us return," I said, and I lifted us out of the place of cages and bars.

We walked along the boulevard in silence, until Quincy broke it.

"Amelia, there is something that I would ask of you." His voice was low. I knew that what would follow was something serious.

I lay my head on his shoulders, feeling as though a mortal woman might. Just vulnerable enough to want to be surrounded by his deep, masculine presence.

"You have endeared me enough to you that I will acquiesce. What is it?"

"Only the barest sentiment of endearment? Come now, Amelia, surely you feel some deeper stirrings of affection?"

"Do not try my patience, human. I neither want nor care for love." I glanced up at him, my gaze hardening.

"Not even if this human has the barest stirrings of deeper affection for you?"

A flutter in my chest.

That could not be right. I did not have a heart to flutter.

"Worse and worse. State what it is."

Quincy ran a hand through his hair, a trait that I was beginning to adore. He cleared his throat. "I was wondering if you might be willing to...dispatch an enemy. He prowls the streets and has been murdering women for many weeks."

I laughed from my belly.

"Quincy, you realize that I kill humans? I drink their blood and leave them dry."

Finally, something to make him blanch.

"Not like this," he said quietly. "Besides, have you ever considered...well, *not* killing humans?"

Again, a burble of laughter escaped my throat. "And deny my nature? My very existence?" A thread of anger slipped down my spine. "Are you trying to tell me what to do?"

"Not at all. But what I am saying is: would you kill me?"

"No." The word was automatic.

"Why not?"

"Well, I enjoy your company. You manage not to be the dullest creature on earth."

"High praise from a vampire. Why else?"

"Well, I suppose I would think it wrong to kill someone with whom I've shared a bed."

"Floor and cushions," Quincy corrected me. "Just think about humans the same way you think of me."

I scowled. That would not be easy.

"And," Quincy continued. "If you have such self-control as you say, then perhaps you can start taking only small amounts of blood at a time. Do not drain humans all in one go."

My face softened. It did possess a semblance of sense.

"If you feel that you must kill, I will not deny your nature. I cannot ask the tiger to remove its claws nor fangs, nor do I ask you to do the same. Only...perhaps you can limit yourself to other murderers. Like this person." Quincy lowered his voice again. "They're calling him the Ripper. Really, Amelia, he—" his voice caught in his throat. "He rips them open. For nothing. You kill to feed. Nothing more drives this man than pure evil."

He lifted my fingers to his lips. A rush went through me down to my toes. A dizzying, magnificent, worrying rush. "Find him. Stop him. Please."

Light was about to crack over the surface of the earth.

I stood up on my toes to kiss Quincy on the lips. "This I will do—for you."

Chapter 24

When I woke the following night, I began to prowl the underbelly of London. No more sweet flowers and delicate trees here—only a malevolent, green fog permeating everything. Through the haze I walked, and my mind turned to the man called Quincy.

Something drew me to him, although I could not say precisely what. I wanted to believe that it was only his form, his physique. Those years in the military had chiseled and carved his muscles to perfection. His chest was broad and hard, and his abs rippled to perfection. I was half-tempted to turn him right then and there, to preserve that flawlessness for all eternity. Then I remembered viciously that Victor said that I could not turn another human.

What if that was a lie? I thought, then dismissed it. Whatever Victor was, he was not a liar when it came to our abilities. In that, I had always trusted him.

So then, what was it about Quincy?

My groin ached pleasantly and deeply whenever I thought of our tryst—and I thought of it often. I only felt slightly guilty in having Quincy as a distraction from Victor. I knew where my heart really was.

He is a distraction, nothing more, I thought, as I passed prostitutes and pickpockets. *Something to keep my mind busy while I scheme how to kill Victor's new woman. To keep my mind off Victor himself.*

But, something did not feel right with that thought. I could choose any man for a simple distraction, screw him, drain him, and leave him for dead. But with Quincy, I wanted more. For the first time, I wanted to be more. For hundreds of years, I had been the perfect killing creature, honed to excellence. But Quincy had suggested that I would use my urges to help humanity.

In the fog and shadows, I scoffed.

Ha.

Help humanity.

What a joke.

Then what was it that I could not ignore? What made my lifeless heart beat for him, for the thought of him? Why did I want to taste his lips again, run my fingers through his hair, show him all the darkest parts of myself? I told him things that I swore I would keep secret for eternity, and I, more than most people, knew how very long eternity was.

It is his bravery, I thought. *His sheer audacity to look death in the eye and laugh.*

That sort of willingness to let go of everything was astounding in a human.

I had not responded to Quincy's comment about the tiger in the cage, because the dreamy effects of opium had still flowed through me, and I was floating on a cloud of happiness and contentment from our carnal delights. However, when I thought about the seemingly-innocuous comment, I balked, and not a little at that. Who was he to suggest that I was in a cage, much less that I kept myself there? Did I not free myself from the castle? Did I not travel half the globe to hunt down my jailer?

Cage indeed.

And his comment about not draining humans dry? Hmpf. He claimed to be without the intention of controlling me, but some part of my mind thought that he was exactly like the other humans: they only wanted to keep wild beasts as pets, to gaze upon when the fancy struck and to ignore at will.

But he is different, and you know it, said a small voice within.

I quickly ground a mental heel against that little vermin and turned to my task: find the killer of the women. My first thought was that it was Victor, but Quincy had shown me the pictures in the papers. Victor wanted to turn other women into fellow companions of undead, not to slash them open. Besides, it was not Victor's style; he was elegant and poised in all things. The mess I saw in the pictures could only be the work of an uncouth human.

I turned a corner in the dark alley and nearly ran straight into the mumbling, crazy man I had met before. He was just as filthy, but this time, at least his beard was shaved, and he had a clean face.

If anyone would know about the evil happenings, it would be this street rat, I thought.

Grabbing his collar, I pulled him against a building.

"Good evening, Mr. Renfield at your service," the man half-giggled. His voice was high and squeaky.

"Lunatic, tell me what you know about the murders of the women," I demanded. My fists held his collar tightly, and I gave him a little shake.

"Master, master!" he cried out. He sounded like a peeping mouse.

"Your master cannot save you now."

"No, my lady, no," Renfield giggled again. "You misunderstand. My master follows yours. The good Dr. Seward follows the one called Victor. He wanted me to kill the women. He made me do it."

"You are sure of this?"

The man's head lolled from side to side. "Quite sure, quite sure. The tall man with black hair, your master, isn't he? He gave me the knife to use. He wants us to do it. I tried to tell him no, but my master is harsh."

I relaxed my hands. The man fidgeted with his hands, glancing this way and that. I knew enough of humans to know that he wanted to confess something more.

"What else do you know?" I tightened my fists again.

The man mumbled something.

"Speak up!"

"Lord Holmwood, I said! My master also killed the Lord Holmwood! He was driven by rage and jealousy."

I knew not of this Holmwood, nor did I care about him. My only concern was the missing women.

I gave him another shake. "Take me to your master."

Then, a most peculiar chance came over the man. His eyes lost the dim look that they had. His head straightened, and his eyes at once became brighter.

"He is closer than you think," he said in a deep, low voice.

Then his hands clamped over my wrists.

I cried out in pain.

This man had a grip like an iron vise. He twisted his arms, and in one fluid motion, he had my arms pinned behind my back.

With one hand, he grabbed a fistful of my hair and slammed my head against the building behind me. The rough brick grazed my cheek, and I cried out. With the other, he held my arm pinned against my back, jerking it skyward. The pain in my shoulder was horrendous.

By the devil, he is strong, I thought, my eyes filling with tears.

I tried to move, but I was horribly pinned. Then, he leaned in close to my ear, his foul breath filling my nostrils. He whispered, "Just as your master is near you."

Then he fled.

By the time I turned around, all that remained was the dismal, green fog.

Chapter 25

I stalked back to the brothel, where I knew that Quincy would be waiting for me. The night was almost gone, and I would have to tell Quincy what had happened the following night. It was a good thing. London was becoming my second home. I know knew the streets like I knew the stars above, like I knew the sound of every animal who stalked in the darkness. I wanted to wrap myself in that darkness and wear it like a shroud. Perhaps stay in my coffin for a few decades.

I was completely and utterly humiliated.

How did that human get the better of me? That thought circled around in my head, with each click of my boot against the pavement. *How?*

He had been brutally strong. Stronger than any mortal had the right to be. Only one being held that sort of strength, and that was Victor.

As if by simply thinking of him, I summoned him. I heard slow, even clapping echo through the streets.

"Bravo," he said, stepping into the greasy light of the streetlamps. "I don't think I've seen anyone beaten that quickly before."

I gave a half-hearted snarl. If any moment was the right time to kill Victor, it was then. I wanted to wipe that stupid smirk from his face once and for all.

But shame is a heavy burden, and I did not feel, as Quincy would say, a worthy opponent for him. I wanted to beat him when I was not exhausted. If I were honest with myself, I still did not want to see him snuffed from this life completely, but then again, I had always wanted to craft a rich, delicious chocolate cake and eat it too, slice by slice. Besides that, I still needed to find the woman that he wanted to turn. I would kill her, in front of Victor, and watch as he realized that, for once, I had bested him, then kill him.

I'm sorry Quincy, I thought. I will find your killer, but first I must do this one last thing.

Perhaps I would eventually stop killing humans, as Quincy suggested. But first, the one that Victor wanted.

"What's the matter?" Victor said from the shadows. The tall buildings threw disfigured shadows against each other. I stopped walking and turned my head to the sound. When I looked forward again, he had appeared before me. "Human caught hold of your tongue?"

Stepping around him, I rolled my eyes. Victor would have to try harder than that. The mention of Quincy had put his face in my mind. All I wanted was to return to him and lick my wounds in the solace of the candlelight and the lush pillows that we had laid on. I was beginning to feel that Victor was not even worth my time to be upset about.

"What I do with my tongue is no concern of yours, anymore."

"Ho, ho, look who is feisty tonight. Have you forgotten that you are still part of this family?" He leapt in front of me, stopping me in my tracks. He crossed his arms in front of him.

"You broke apart the family when you left." This time, I walked past him, intentionally brushing my shoulder against his. I no longer feared him as I did before. "Therefore, there is no family to belong to."

"Hmm, such a shame. I'm bringing on a lovely little blonde. Hair is golden like angels' wings, with eyes the color of the morning sky you'll never see again. Truly, you two will have such fun. She is as sweet as spring, and you..." His eyes flicked over my body. "Well, you are the night to her day. She will remind you of summer." He gave a soft little sigh, and I wished I had kept the knife I had given to Quincy, so I could plunge it in his heart. "Just think of it: her name means "light." I've never met someone with such a delicious name."

"Bon appetit."

I kept walking. Victor could not hurt me now.

He hurried to keep up with me. "So, do you like my little puppet?"

"Yes, my lover has asked for me to cut his strings."

"Lover! Quite so. You *are* falling for him, aren't you?"

I curled my lip in response. "What use do you have for him, anyway?"

"Besides to keep you occupied, while I turn my dear light-bringer into the world of darkness?"

Something began to click in my mind about what Victor had said about the name of the woman. But it retreated, like a dream upon waking, and it had been so very long since I dreamed.

"Not *Quincy*." I rubbed my still-throbbing shoulder. "Your minion."

"Ah yes. The mad scientist type. Well, *someone* has to take the fall for women disappearing. It just so happens that he has an ax to grind against women of poor moral character. As long as the spotlight is one someone ripping and murdering women, I am free to pick and choose as I please."

"His days are numbered. As are yours."

"I'm positively quivering." He brushed a strand of hair behind my ears. "Just as your legs do when I've taken you in every imaginable way."

I couldn't help it. A low throb pounded insistently against my groin.

"Tell me, do you think your human will keep you occupied? Do you think he can please you the way I can?"

Heat flooded my face. If I had had circulating blood, I would have blushed. Victor continued, relentless. "Do you think that he can handle you? That human is nothing but straw to your steel. Do you think that you can be anything than what you are, a huntress?"

Victor looked at the sky. "Until the next night."
And then he was gone.

Chapter 26

When Quincy heard that Lucy had died, he was devastated. Any remaining romantic interest that he had in her had vanished. His sole focus now was on Amelia. She had taken his heart from him, stolen it right beneath his ribs, and it was possible that she did not even know it. Amelia was all he could think about over the course of the past several weeks.

Still, Lucy had been his friend. He still cared for her, now in a platonic way, and his heart broke for poor Arthur as well.

They gathered in the graveyard for her funeral. The day was gray and wet, as a miserable rain fell and chilled them to the bone. Their breath fogged in the air, as they huddled beneath black umbrellas. Arthur stood next to Dr. Seward, and someone who Quincy did not recognize. Mina, too, was there, openly weeping, while Jonathan, whose hair had gone positively white, stood beside her, clutching her hand.

*If only Mina knew...*he thought.

He remembered Amelia's words to him. Jonathan had been a pawn of this...Victor. An immortal vampire that wanted to expand his "family."

Quincy shivered. From Amelia's description, he knew that he had encountered Victor that night in the slums. He had known something was evil about him.

The priest began the funeral sermon, and Quincy felt only mildly guilty that he could not focus on the dry, meaningless words. He had not known Lucy and was no more fit to give the last words than a stranger off the street. Furthermore, religion had begun to lose its appeal for Quincy. Amelia was a vampire, and so she was not among the living. But she could still die. Did that mean that she had a soul? Was there a God who cared about such things?

Besides, Amelia had rocked his entire world off center. She stood for everything that was mysterious and feral in the world. She was fierce, wild, intelligent, and daring. Perhaps even a little broken, even if she did not realize it. He had never met another being like Amelia.

That thought scared Quincy. He did not fear that she would harm him. She did not fear to die. Only to lose her.

They would bury Lucy in a family sepulcher. The coffin would be place in a stone sarcophagus and then placed in a wall of stone. After the service, everyone placed a white rose upon the coffin. Quincy was not ashamed to cry for his friend, who he had once thought to marry.

After the funeral, everyone met at Arthur Holmwood's estate in the country, to give their condolences. It was an opulent mansion, with sixteen rooms, and towering arches. The white marble was flecked with orange and red, and the engravings depicted cherubs alongside demons. Mina's mouth practically gaped when she and Jonathan rode up in the carriage with Quincy. The gravel leading to the front door was immaculately tidy, and rose bushes trimmed the drive. Their sweet scent reminded Quincy of Amelia, and as much as he was despondent over the passing of Lucy, he could not wait to return to her arms. Whatever detail she mentioned about herself, he had to know more. He recognized something in Amelia that he identified: a huntress. He did not criticize her desire for human blood, because it was all she had ever known.

Perhaps she can come to use her...gift...in a way that helps people, he thought.

It was a wild hope, he knew. Still, wild hopes befit a wild woman.

Once he had feared that he would not find a nice, genteel lady. It was all that he had dreamed of in Africa. As he had stood outside, smoking a rare pipe, gazing at the diamond-filled sky, he had dreamed that he would find a nice society lady, someone who could cook and darn and do all the things that ladies were supposed to do. All he had wanted to was fall in line in his place in life.

But Africa had changed him. Amelia had changed him. Both had given him a hunger for the things that he could not control, could never control. Most people ran from danger, from tempests, and earthquakes, predators, and bullets. Not Quincy. He welcomed it with open arms, because he had seen what it was like to respect something so much that he greatest honor would be to die by its hand.

Or, rather, its paw, in the case of the lion.

Amelia was none of the things he had wanted. She was more. He suddenly realized that he would follow her, wherever she went. However much or little time they had together.

And he lov—

"Thank you all for coming today," said Arthur, interrupting Quincy's thoughts. "I want to introduce my associate. Dr. Seward helped me find him. It is possible that he has information regarding the murders that we have all seen in the papers lately. And Lucy."

Arthur had mentioned something about this mysterious newcomer, with a thin, white beard, and round spectacles. Everyone's ears pricked at the mention of Lucy's name.

"I thought Lucy suffered from a wasting disease," said Quincy. He did indeed feel guilty, just then.

I should have paid more attention to her, he thought. *But Amelia...*

"So did I," said Dr. Seward. "But when I discovered that Lucy was having nightly hallucinations and displayed a strong dislike toward the light, I began to wonder. I wrote my associate, Dr. Van Helsing."

The older man gave a curt nod to everyone around the room as he took the floor.

"Beloved friends of Lucy, I am here to tell you that I believe that her affliction was something more than mere wasting. It was...other worldly," said Van Helsing.

Mina's brow furrowed. "How do you mean, Mr. Van Helsing?"

"Doctor." He cleared his throat. "And I mean that there is a creature of evil stalking the poor women of London at this moment. This creature is so evil that nothing matters to it. He is neither dead nor alive, and his is stronger than all of us combined."

Quincy suddenly swallowed. He began to raise his voice to denounce Victor and what he knew.

"I believe he has an accomplice," continued Van Helsing. "Possibly another of the undead."

The words that Quincy was about to utter caught in his throat. He closed his mouth. Dr. Seward looked sharply at him, but said nothing.

Amelia.

"And how does this connect with our dear Lucy?" said Mina.

Dr. Van Helsing took off his spectacles and began to clean them. "She is currently transforming into one of them. One of the undead. A vampire."

Quincy's heart started to pound. Lucy? Becoming one of Victor's brood? From all that Amelia had told him, Victor deserved to die. Amelia had been caught and captured against her will. But Victor...Victor was the source of the evil.

And yet, even as the thought crossed his mind, Quincy remained in silence. Amelia was looking for the killer of the women. He now knew it was Victor. Surely she would choose to do good, follow the path of choosing right over evil?

Or was she already damned?

For the rest of the afternoon, they talked about "the vampire's" various strengths and weaknesses. Quincy did not know whether the half of it was true. He would have to ask Amelia. Still, one thing was certain, they were all destined to meet tomorrow in the graveyard, to put Lucy's soul to rest once and for all.

"At midnight. That is when the moon will be at its peak. If she is to turn into...one of them...it will be at that time."

Whatever may happen, she does not deserve to live with Victor for the rest of eternity, thought Quincy.

"When do we meet?" asked Mina. Her eyes were flecked with tears, but her gaze steely. Quincy thought that he had never seen a friend as loyal as Mina. He would never tell her what had passed between Jonathan and Amelia. Quincy understood why he had fallen into temptation. He understood all too well with Amelia.

When they were finished shaking hands, and bidding their farewells, Dr. Seward took him to the side.

"Quincy," Dr. Seward said, gripping his arm.

The man is strong for his age, thought Quincy. *Perhaps it is the passion to find the killer that gives him that strength.*

The doctor's fingers dug into Quincy's arm. "Do you know anything more about these murders or this evil that lives among us?" he asked, his gaze boring into Quincy's.

Quincy did not even dare think about Amelia. He tried to keep his mind completely blank, even though he could hear his blood whooshing through his ears. To say something would put her in danger of being hunted.

"No," he replied evenly. "I only wish I did."

The doctor looked Quincy up and down. "Indeed. Well, if you discover anything more, be sure to contact me. I'm always ready, day or night."

"Of course, doctor, of course."

Dr. Seward withdrew his hand.

"Good. Because if anyone were hiding any information, I would hate to think that it would cause...*danger*, to our mission."

Quincy was suddenly terrified.

Chapter 27

I met Quincy again at the brothel, the scarlet room with beeswax candles becoming very comforting and familiar. The bed now seemed an open invitation, calling to us, but Quincy was positively vibrating with unspoken words. How handsome he looked just then, his dark hair falling into his eyes, the cut of his shirt pulling across his wide shoulders. He looked so tasty that I wanted to lick every inch of him. It did not help that I had not fed in several days, and I could feel my thirst building inside me, lining my throat with fire and my belly with need.

He was pacing back and forth, just as the caged lion had in the zoo, while I sat on the luxuriously soft mattress. I kept glancing to the throbbing vein in his neck, and I struggled to pull my thoughts to the present.

"They are gathering to attack," he said. "A man named Van Helsing has caught wind that there are vampires in the city. They will all go to the graveyard tonight to put Lucy's soul to rest. But they are planning on hunting down you and Victor. They think that you are behind the deaths of the women."

I waved a hand away. "They are not worth caring about. I do not fear humans, and I never have."

But Quincy merely shook his head. "You do not understand. This man, Van Helsing, he has weapons, knowledge. In his bid to find and destroy Victor, he could find and destroy you."

I smiled at Quincy, like a mother whose child was being petulant. I was sure that there was nothing to fear from these humans.

"Even so," I said. "I bring news of the one you wanted to find. The killer of women. He is the unfortunate creature of your friend, Dr. Seward. He is mad but of incredible strength." I rubbed my shoulder remembering the pain he had inflicted.

Quincy turned his head sharply to me. "You confronted him? What happened?"

I felt a renewed heat flood my cheeks. "As I said, the devil is incredibly strong. Too strong. No human could naturally have the strength he does."

Quincy stared at me, without a trace of judgement in his eyes.

"I accosted him in the streets. He confessed that he had murdered the women, but at the behest of his master, Dr. Seward. He said that he was merely a creature of the doctor's wishes," I continued.

Quincy sharply inhaled. He closed his eyes as though receiving a blow. "Dr. Seward ordered him to kill the women. But why?"

I shrugged, adopting the very human gesture I had picked up from Quincy. "That I cannot say. I was going to put the poor creature out of his earthly misery, but..." I swallowed. He had changed, god damn him. Something had peaked through the madness, an icy clarity that betrayed the full depths of his evil. "...but I could not hold him. He slipped from my grasp and escaped."

But Quincy only shook his head again. "I cannot believe it...Dr. Seward. And his creature, Renfield. I saw him, with Victor. Victor was giving him a knife of some sort. I knew it was evil, some dark pact. But what has Dr. Seward to do with Victor?" He put his head in his hands, as if to stop the swirling thoughts within. He came to sit next to me on the bed and turned to me.

Refusing to give into the desire to hang my head in shame, I looked Quincy in the eyes.

The bedsheets rustled beneath us, as we adjusted ourselves.

"I wonder..." said Quincy. "What might it be like, to feel what you feel? To be what you are?" He paused. "Perhaps I can protect you."

Slowly, so slowly that I almost didn't notice, my body began to tense. Lock in a sort of faint readying for battle.

"What do you mean?" I asked, even though I knew exactly what he meant. Dreaded his response.

"To be a vampire," he replied. He then lifted my chin to gaze into his eyes. "I want to be with you. I want you more than I've wanted anything in my entire life, and only you can give me that."

I tried to scoff and brush off his words. "Let me get you a glass of wine," I said, starting to get up.

But he locked his hands around my waist, pulling me closer. "Think of it," he whispered. "You and I. Together." He paused, and again, bade me to turn around and look at him. "Change me. Make me a vampire."

This time I did laugh.

"You do not know what you ask," I said. "Even if it could be done, I would not. Not to you, nor anyone. You are too soft. Too human." I turned my face away and thought of the endless trail of death that followed my footsteps.

"I am not afraid of death," he said. "I am a hunter."

"No," I said. "You know what it is to kill an animal, but could you kill one of your fellow humans?"

Quincy remained silent.

Perhaps, in the back of my mind, I wanted to protect Quincy, just as he wanted to protect me. But all I could think of was Victor's words, saying that only he held the power of transformation.

I changed the subject back to the madman, Renfield.

"But I shall finish the work that you asked of me. I will hunt him down, this man Renfield. I will do this, for you."

"No," he said, as though answering his own thoughts. "Now I cannot let you become embroiled in this anymore. I cannot let you risk your life for me. I cannot let you hunt him."

My annoyance sprung sharp and quick.

"Let me?" I said. "Let me? There is very little—if anything—you can allow me to do or not do."

I pulled away from him, sprang from the bed, which I had been eyeing with ever-growing concentration.

"I didn't mean—"

"Do not presume to tell me what to do."

"If you try to hunt Seward's creature, then they could hurt you," said Quincy, as he walked toward me. "They could kill you!"

"And? What if it is my time to die?"

We were both fairly shouting. Our faces were barely a hair's breadth apart.

He suddenly grabbed my arms. "Do not say that. Don't."

"And why not?"

"Because I love you, dammit!"

Quincy's chest heaved with the exertion of his breath. My own breath was snatched away from me.

He cupped my cheek in his hand, a tender gesture that belied the storm forming between us, within us.

"I love you, and I cannot bear the thought of anything happening to you," he whispered. Then he placed both hands against my face and drew me to him. He kissed me, powerfully, irresistibly. We were two opposites, drawn together with all the force of a magnet.

His ragged groan filled the room, inciting my instincts. It was the sound of prey wounded, of giving in, of complete surrender, and my fangs lowered in response. I did not think that I would be able to resist him this night.

Not after what he had said.

He had now given himself to me, I knew. He offered up the best and worst of himself, without expecting anything in return.

Tears would have come to my eyes, if not for Quincy's hands fiercely pulling me closer to him, letting his tongue slip deeper into my mouth. I felt a pull deep in my belly, a hot desire growing stronger with every lash of his skilled tongue. When he felt my sharp incisors, he gasped, as he cut his tongue slightly on one of them. He pulled back just an instant, and I grinned wickedly at him, my fangs fully extended.

The tiny bit of blood that had crept from his tongue to mine electrified me. There was no stopping the wildness within. But still, I held off as long as I could, not just to increase the pleasure when I finally gave in. There was still a tiny part of me that was clenching to something in the past, afraid to let go completely. Sharing blood was one of the most intimate things a vampire could do, with anyone.

I looked at him dead in the eye. "Afraid?" I asked, panting with desire for him, his body, and his blood.

"Not hardly."

We fell together once more, in a furious race to see who could plant more kisses on the other.

I felt my body go at once deliciously heavy with desire and light with the knowledge that this man, who I was slowly coming to adore, loved me.

Our clothes were soon torn off and thrown to the ground. Quincy stroked my breasts with every-growing urgency, and he bent his head to take a nipple in his sweet mouth. As he sucked and teased, energy shot through me, and I felt myself become more alive than I had been in centuries. I raked my nails down his shoulders and back, and he cried out in agonized pleasure.

Quincy stroked between my thighs, groaning in that deep, masculine way of his, when he felt that I was ready for him. He pushed my legs apart with his, and I opened willingly for him. With one hand on his erect member and one on my leg, he stroked himself as he looked at me.

I crooked a finger at him, grinning.

He drove himself into me, filling me to the very sheath. We came together in a frenzy, rocking, finding that powerful rhythm that we were both quickly learning in each other. My body responded to every quiver and pulse of his. My breath came faster and harder as he dipped and thrust into me.

My pleasure and excitement were quickly growing. Quincy seemed to sense it, and he bared his neck for me.

"Do it," he commanded. "Take me. Drink from me."

I could smell his sweet scent as the blood pounded through him; it seemed to match the pounding of my heart.

This was it; my ultimate challenge and desire, the thing that I wanted most in the world, and could not give back once taken. Quincy did not know what he asked, but then if he did, he might not have done so. Still, the thought of conquering, of dominated him in this way so excited me, that my body convulsed, and I reached the release I needed.

At the peak of my desire, I sank my fangs into him.

The world went white for both of us. This was the only time that I could see light that was as bright as day that would not harm me. It was neither warm nor cool, but simply *was*. An eternal being, made out of the purest love, the purest desire. We were floating in a sea of arousal, perfectly calm, perfectly poised. Our bodies filled with the knowledge of each other, as our minds opened completely. I saw his heart, his hopes, his desires. I saw his fears, and I knew he saw mine. But we were perfectly relaxed, perfectly calm, hovering in this blanket of security and warmth. The very air around us, whatever ether we were floating in, seemed to throb and pulse with the erotic sensations we know both felt.

My body, wherever it was, for surely our spirits had left them now, as we hovered high above the earth, pulled and sucked at the salty, rich blood. I felt it go down my throat, delicious, fulfilling but frustrating, as I could fill my need now, but always with the knowledge that the thirst would come again. I felt it flow through my veins, restoring the life that I could no longer be a part of.

I saw Quincy emerge through the whiteness, that beautiful, pearlescent sheen, and I knew that I loved him. I knew it, but even in that delightful zone of sleep and waking, I could not tell him. One last string tugged at my heart, and I did not know how to release it. Still, I tried to. I opened up my mind and body to try to tell him what I could not with words.

Suddenly, I felt Quincy's heart pounding in my ears. He would die soon, if I did not stop. I had taken all that I could, without killing him.

I released him at once, and as I did, I felt as though my spirit were falling heavily back to earth.

Snapping my eyes open, I looked at Quincy, the candlelight seeming so much dimmer than the brightness of the white light. In the aftermath, he could not speak, so spent he was. I wanted to fetch him some broth and good, strong wine, to help him regain his strength, but...I lay my head on his chest, his heart beating weakly beneath. I snuggled closer to him, wanting to cling to that level that we had felt when I had sunk my fangs into him. Tremors of remembered pleasure pulsed through us still, and we did not speak for a long time.

He wrapped me closer to him, and I thought that if there were any such thing as happiness, it was right here with Quincy. He could move me in so many ways, and most surprisingly of all was with tenderness. He had confessed his love to me, and I in returned had opened myself to him in one of the deepest ways possible.

> Quincy kissed the top of my head, and I felt myself relax even further against his chest. He cleared his throat. "So, have you ever done that? Bitten anyone, I mean."

I gazed at his hands, so strong, so filled with promise in the candlelight, with its fingers intertwined in mine.

"No," I replied, completely un-self-conscious, completely open to him. "Never. You are the first, the only, the singular."

Quincy chuckled, deep in his throat. "I enjoyed it. I enjoyed watching you, as well."

Suddenly, the fog in my brain vanished. I felt my stomach tightened, and I did not know whether to feel savage glee or torment. I suddenly knew who Victor's new pursuit was, who he wanted to turn into a new vampire.

Just think of it: her name means "light."

Light.

Lucy.

Immediately, I flew off the bed.

Quincy sat up, looking puzzled. "Amelia, what's wrong?"

Dress, boots, cloak, all of it, I had thrown on in half a blink.

"There is something that I must do," I responded, yanking my laces tight. The boots lovingly cupped my calves, and I loved the tight feel of leather around my feet. It made me feel as though I were ready to face anything.

Quincy may have been a human, but he was no fool.

"You're going to the cemetery, aren't you?" He threw off the covers of the bed. I did not have time to admire his polished physique.

I said nothing. I didn't have to. I didn't have to explain myself to anybody, much less this human. Even though, this human was growing on me. Even though we had told each other things in the night that I cupped to my heart like precious jewels.

He got up and tried to block the door. "Don't go," he begged.

I laughed. "Are you trying to block my path? Get out of my way."

He didn't budge.

"Quincy, don't be a fool. Move."

He suddenly looked as though he were a child and I had taken away his favorite toy. His bottom lip quivered slightly. "Amelia, if you go, you are in danger of being killed. They are gathering there tonight to dispatch Lucy. She will go to her eternal rest, no matter what. But if you go, you will face the danger of death." He moved toward me and gripped my arms. "Don't you see? I love you. And I cannot bear the thought of anything happening to you."

The words hit me like falling hailstones from the sky.

Of all the things that Victor had said to me, not once, not ever, had he uttered those words. Oh, he lusted after me, and we loved to titillate each other, but he had never cared for me in the way that Quincy had.

"Idiot," I whispered. "I have to do this. I don't care if they are planning on killing her. I have to be the one to drive the knife into her heart." My eyes filled with tears, stained red. "She matters to Victor."

Pain sliced across Quincy's face. "Just come back to the bed," he whispered. "Forget about Victor. Forget about them all. Just come back and stay with me." He gripped my arm tighter. "Please."

Perhaps I would have, if he had not grabbed my arm. Perhaps I would have, if he had not constantly been trying to tell me what to do, trying to control me. I would not be controlled any longer.

And I would prove that by killing Victor's precious Lucy.

Chapter 28

NECROPOLIS

That word hung like an ax over the arched entrance to the cemetery. The night was as black as a witch's cat's fur, and I easily bent the iron bars that formed the gate, until I made a space large enough for my body to pass through.

Mist clung to the ground and swirled around my ankles as I walked over the remains of the dead.

Lucy.

No last name. I didn't know that. No matter, I would find her. Her body would be in a grave freshly dug or else a sepulcher with wet cement plastering the hole.

Suddenly, I heard voices. I slunk behind one of the towering trees, evading tombstones and statues of angels, whose faces had been corroded by time.

"And how do you know that she is here?" said a voice.

"She will be. If she is just-turned into one of the Undead, then her powers will be weaker. She will not be able to rise at sundown, with sunlight still filtering through the night, as some of the older ones can. No, she will be in her coffin." The voice sounded studious and elegant, but there was power in it that came from years of wisdom.

Quincy's hunting party. I had to get there first.

I raced along the ground, my steps quieted by years of hunting. No twigs snapped beneath my feet and no grass rustled to give away my position to the other humans.

In my rage, I had neglected to bring along the one thing that could kill us: a means of fire.

But, I saw a faint light bobbing and weaving in the dim haze. The light was thrown in all directions, giving off an orangey glow, that made everything around it look like it came from the inside of a pumpkin. Perhaps that would be my means.

There. A huge offering of fresh flowers adorned a small, stone sepulcher. The edifice looked like a small house, with four walls and a little roof, big enough for a few coffins to be placed within its walls. Portraits of the woman I know knew to be Lucy stood next to the bright but decaying flowers. Their sweet smell seemed ghastly to me, for though they were fresh, they were dying. I entered through the doorway and stood inside the small tomb.

Lucy Westenra. Her name was chiseled over the final resting place. I broke open the seal that marked her, and with one hand, pulled out the heavy coffin. I lifted the lid.

She did look quite pretty. Her golden hair fell in ringlets around her heart-shaped face, and her lips were rosy with fresh blood. She must have drunk the night before. As she slept the deep sleep of the dead, I wondered if in some other life, we might have been friends. Sisters. Family.

But that life is not mine, I thought. You are the reason that is driving Victor away from us. Away from me.

Her head needed to be removed, then her body set on fire. Having a knife would make removing her despicably-beautiful head easier, but I was strong. I lifted my hands to their task.

"That's quite far enough," said an all-too-familiar voice.

Victor.

I whipped around, my hands out like claws.

"On the contrary, not nearly," I replied.

He extended his hand to me. "Come. Enough of this foolish jealousy. Lucy is in the final throes of transition. You will to back to Transylvania tonight, and you will bring her with you."

"No," I said. When had I ever disobeyed Victor? When had I ever been brave enough or strong enough to follow my own desires?

"The grave! Someone is there!" Other voices whispered in the darkness. To Victor and I, with our keen senses, they seemed as loud as bugles.

A shadow flitted over the doorway, as a human blocked out the light of the moon. A man with white hair and spectacles stood, holding a crossbow.

"Vampire," he hissed, lifting the crossbow.

He fired.

Victor and I darted to the sides of the confining sepulcher. The arrow embedded itself into the wall. I whipped my head around and lifted my hands in defense.

Even Victor could see the vulnerability of being inside the house-like structure. He ran out the doorway, to attack the humans.

And left me alone with his precious Lucy.

That was his mistake, thinking that I would blindly follow him until the end of time. That I would simply go along with whatever he thought of, simply because he was Victor, my maker. Part of me wanted that, as well. It would be so simple if I could just give him whatever he wanted, when he wanted.

But after five hundred years, something broke in me.

Perhaps I should have ran or fought off the humans, but now was my opportunity. I picked up the metal-tipped arrow, savoring its sharp point, then plunged it into her heart. Then, ripping it free, I liberated her head from its delicate neck.

Blood sprayed everywhere, and I thought I caught a familiar scent in its bouquet, but in the heat of the moment, I could not place it. I gripped Lucy's head by her hair and walked to the entrance of the tomb.

I thought I would feel different, but I don't, I managed to think in a haze. I had been hunting down Lucy for so long, and now that she was dead, finally and truly dead, I felt...nothing.

That scared me more than the arrow fired from the crossbow or staying out too late, close to dawn. I tried to give myself a slap, as humans do when they want to return feeling to hands or feet numbed by cold. But nothing came.

I looked down at the head clutched in my fingers, and I realized that killing Victor's woman had done nothing for me. My pain and torment still raged.

Stepping outside, I saw the melee between Victor and the humans. They were desperately trying to kill him, while he flitted through the cemetery, toying with them, teasing them as a cat does.

"Come now, plaything, let's see what you have," cried Victor to Quincy. Victor weaved in and out of the humans, batting them, pushing them, trying to get them to make a mistake. Everyone: Quincy, the older man with white hair, the man I recognized as Jonathan, and two others I did not recognize were armed to the teeth with knives, arrows, and guns, all laced with silver metal, no doubt. That metal would not kill us, but it would slow us down and hurt mightily. One man looked vaguely familiar, but I could not place him in my mind.

"Victor!" I yelled. I held up the head so he could see, then simply let it drop. I turned to Quincy. "Do you see," I said, my voice in a daze. "I can never be what you want me to be. I will never be more than a killer."

Quincy doubled over as though he had been physically punched in the gut. A part of me was sorry that he had to see his friend this way, but I was too blinded by my own need to hurt Victor. Tears made Quincy's eyes shiny. He reached up with both hands to place them against the sides of his head, as though trying to keep his mind whole, by sheer force of will.

Upon seeing the ghastly vision of his newly-formed spawn in pieces, Victor's face changed expressions to maniacal glee to something I was completely unprepared for:

Grief.

His face twisted in sadness and despair as the truth of what I had done sank into him.

Everyone paused for just a moment, but the moment hung like a bubble suspended in the air. I could see Quincy's shocked face, as he looked at my own, blood-streaked one. The white-haired man's lips were set in grim determination. Jonathan looked both terrified and pained. The wind rustled through the leaves and brought with it the smell of rain. Clouds drifted over the moon and plunged us all into deeper darkness. My other fist still clutched the arrow, and blood gleamed off the shiny metal.

I lifted the arrow to my teeth to taste it. I had an overpowering curiosity to know what this Lucy had tasted like.

Ugh. Horrible. Dead man's blood.

But still, there was an undercurrent, that wonderful, citrus-y zest that set off a recollection in my mind that I still could not place. I knew that I had tasted it before, but it was overpowered by the putrid stench of rot. Once the body dies, the blood is noxious to vampires, toxic if much time has passed between the death and the imbibing.

Victor jerked his head up, and the moment broke.

The humans watched in fright, as they saw the unfurling drama between Victor and I. Perhaps they thought we would kill each other.

Perhaps we would.

"You idiot," he whispered. "What have you done?"

We stalked around each other, as adrenaline poured into my veins. I knew then, that Victor and I would fight until one of us was dead.

But then Victor did something that I did not anticipate at all.

He flew towards Quincy.

Victor was mere inches away from him, and he would have ripped out his throat, if I had not stopped him. My body collided with his and we fell to the ground. The impact felt as though I had hit the side of a boulder.

My breath went out of me. Victor threw me from him, and I rolled across the ground, leaves and twigs sticking to me. He managed to lift himself up first, and he stalked toward Quincy again. He must have wanted to frighten Quincy, for he took what seemed like slow, ponderous steps to me, as compared with the strength and speed a vampire has. To Quincy, they must have seemed terrifyingly fast.

I quickly got to my feet and rushed at Victor, throwing my arms around his neck in an effort to choke him.

Our faces were so close that our cheeks touched.

"You killed what was precious to me," he said. "Now I will kill yours."

Victor plunged an elbow into my stomach, and I saw black stars burst in front of my vision, but still I held. I squeezed his neck harder.

"Run, you fool!" I screamed. "Run, all of you!"

The humans, interestingly, stayed where they were. They looked on us with a mixture of grim fascination and horror. To them, it must have seemed like two wild beasts, like lions or wolves fighting.

Victor managed to throw me off him, and we continued to savagely fight.

"Perhaps they will kill each other and spare us the trouble," I heard one of them whisper.

So that was it. They were just waiting until we had fought to the death.

Victor and I might have gone on fighting until the end of time. We laid blow after blow upon each other, neither of us getting the upper hand. Our rage was mutual and fierce, perhaps releasing what had been kept inside us both for five centuries. Yes, we might have done just that, had Victor not leaned in, his breath sweet upon my face, and whispered, "He gave her blood, you know. Quincy. He gave blood to Lucy to save her."

I swear, in that moment, I was suddenly and vividly aware that I had a heart, and that it was breaking. All my breath whooshed out of me, driven from my lungs. Victor's words fell on me harder than any blow that he had landed before.

All my ire, all my rage that could not be contained in words suddenly contracted into one point. I knew that I had to hurt whoever spoke those terrible words.

A glint of silver flashed in the corner of my eye. I sped toward the arrow, lying like a cruel promise on the ground, snatched it up, and plunged it into Victor's chest.

Victor howled, and the sound cut through the high-pitched ringing in my ears. Blinking, my gaze fell on his chest. It was as though I had come out of a daze and only now saw the destruction that I had wrought. In my emotion, I had missed his heart, and now the arrow stuck out of his chest, just below his shoulder.

"To home," Victor said, and I did not know whether he mean it as an invitation for me to follow him or simply a statement. Already, blood was dripping from Victor's mouth, as the silver poisoned his blood. He would need his native earth, the healing that could only come from sleeping deep in the ground of his home.

He fled, leaving me yet again.

I turned to Quincy, the others standing as still as stone. I lifted an accusing finger, although I did not who was the object of my indictment.

"You gave her blood!" I hissed. "Do you know what you have done?"

So *that* was why her blood had tasted familiar. Quincy had given her his and so flowed through her veins.

I grit my teeth against the pain that now ground against my heart. Quincy had shown me the greatest pleasure and greatest pain, in ways that not even Victor had done. For all his speeches and self-aggrandizing, Victor had never known how to hurt me like Quincy now had.

"I go to my master," I said. "One of us will die. If you are brave, you will find him in Transylvania."

Then, I too, fled into the night.

Chapter 29

Quincy knew he faced certain danger in entering Dr. Seward's house. His heart had started beating harder, even before he approached the door. He was perhaps one hundred feet away, when his hunter's instincts pricked. The hair on the back of his neck raised, and he knew that he was being watched. He glanced around, careful to appear carefree, as though surveying what a beautiful day it was. Then, taking out a handkerchief from his pocket, he mopped his face but then let it fall, in a feign. He bent down, pretending to pick up the handkerchief, but really checking that the knife Amelia had given him was strapped to his leg was securely fastened. Quincy had an awful feeling that he would use it soon.

He knew that he had to confront the doctor about his patient. He also knew that Dr. Seward knew about Amelia. Maybe not the specifics, but he knew that Quincy had been cavorting about with a vampire. One of the enemy.

He took a steadying breath and knocked on the door.

A servant opened it, and Quincy entered. Dr. Seward lived in a modest house, but in one of the wealthier parts of London. The furnishings were as elegant as the doctor's accent.

"Quincy," said Dr. Seward, coming into the foyer. His eyes were as hard and glittery as diamonds. "Thank you for coming. I wanted to talk to you in great detail about our...problem."

There was something off about the doctor's voice. Quincy did not know how to explain it, but there was something...unhinged about it. As though the doctor were standing at the very edge of sanity.

They walked into the living room, but both men remained standing. Quincy had never been inside the doctor's house before, as Dr. Seward usually visited his patients and not the other way around. Now, for the first time, Quincy looked about the space: there was medical and scientific equipment everywhere. Beakers and glass bottles held liquids of various colors. Leather-bound notebooks were open, articles from all the latest medical journals and newspapers meticulously stacked one on top of the other. Even now, Quincy heard the faint drip of liquid falling into one of those huge, glass apparatuses, which was placed above a low-burning fire. A stench hung in the air, although Quincy was too polite to remark upon it.

"Indeed," replied Quincy, his heart racing. "We have several to discuss. The first and most pressing is your patient, Renfield."

Just act as though you know nothing, he thought. *Keep your face as still as the surface of a pond.*

"Is that so?" countered the doctor. "I would have thought that the matter of the undead was of most urgent affair."

Was it just Quincy, or had the doctor placed the slightest emphasis on the word "affair?"

"But didn't you see? They fled. One of them said something about Transylvania. With any luck, it was wounded enough that it will die."

The doctor chuckled, a dark sound. He moved closer to the hearth, where the flames burned low. Quincy could feel no warmth coming from them, and he shivered where he stood.

"Don't be naïve, Quincy. They are undead. They cannot die, except by beheading, fire, or sunlight," replied the doctor, picking up the fire poker. He half-heartedly stabbed the embers, but the fire managed to wheeze out a few more sparks, but most of it was already ash. "We must track her. Follow her to the ends of the earth, if we must." The doctor started to put the poker back in the rack but then seemed to think better of it.

"Her?" asked Quincy. "Why only A—the female?"

Dr. Seward noticed the slip and glanced sharply at him.

Quincy swore inwardly but tried to keep his gaze steady. Being in the same room with the doctor now felt as though he was right back in the savannah of Africa, tracking the lion.

"Because, she must die. The other...we might be able to serve him."

"What are you talking about?" Quincy asked, flabbergasted. "He is evil. If anything is to die, it should be him. The male."

Once again, Dr. Seward chuckled. "Come now, Quincy, you and I are men of honor. Let us not pretend to lie anymore. I know that you know the female." Dr. Seward lifted to the poker to his face and inspected the sharpened point, not even looking at Quincy. "I know that you lied to me."

Quincy suddenly felt his stomach clench in fear. Now all his abilities as a hunter came to the fore. Every sound, every smell was sharpened, seemed clear through the drug of adrenaline flowing through him: the dying crackle of fire, the acrid stench of whatever the doctor had over the flame, even the individual fibers of the carpet seemed to stand out in relief.

"Then let us not pretend anymore," said Quincy. "Your patient, Renfield, killed those women, and you covered it up. Perhaps he even killed Lord Holmwood!"

"No," hissed Dr. Seward. "Renfield might have killed those women—yes, he did it. But the honor of killed the honorable Lord Holmwood belongs to me."

Quincy's mouth dropped open. One of his best friends' father...

"What have you done?" whispered Quincy. "Why?"

Dr. Seward smirked. "You should know; you should understand. You were in love with her, too. I could see it in your eyes. We all loved her. It was only with great reluctance that my master convinced me to let him have Lucy," he replied. "I loved her more than anything in the world, and *that traitor*, that...louse—" the doctor now spoke through clenched teeth. "He married her. The jealousy grew in my heart so much that I could not take it. He took the person I loved most in this world from me, so I took the one who mattered the most to him."

Quincy felt the floor begin to give way beneath his feet.

He has lost his mind, Quincy realized.

He tried to stall for time. He would have to process the dark revelation of Holmwood's death later. But he needed to know where Dr. Seward's patient, Renfield, was. He had a connection with Victor. If Quincy knew where Victor might be headed, he could track him, and therefore Amelia. He might be able to save her.

He kept his eyes trained on the doctor, as he walked slowly over to one of his tables; Dr. Seward picked up a tiny vial with a dark blue liquid.

"I got the recipe from my good acquaintance Dr. Jeckell," he said, holding up the vial to the light. "This is a most remarkable recipe. It gives whoever drinks it the strength of ten men."

He downed it in one gulp.

Suddenly, a terrible change came over the doctor. He writhed for a moment and cried out in pain. But after a moment, he composed himself and stood tall.

When he looked back at Quincy, the doctor's face was unchanged, except for the wildness in his eyes.

"Seward!" cried Quincy.

"Just so...or Renfield, whichever I am today," the man said in a high-pitched giggle.

"What?"

Quincy stared aghast at the man who had been his friend, who had been led to the very edge of sanity and fallen through.

"Yes," said the doctor, picking up the fire poker once more. "I am Renfield, and Renfield is me. It is so much easier to kill whenever you can blame it on a crazy patient. But I am not crazy, not Dr. Seward!"

Quincy felt the shock blow through him like wind in a gale. He stretched his mind back to when he had first seen Renfield. It had been dark, and the man had worn a beard. His clothes had been unkempt, and he was dirty, and his hair greasy. He suddenly realized that it had been Dr. Seward all along.

"So you want to kill my master?" he said, suddenly swinging the fire poker at Quincy. "I'm afraid I cannot let you."

And he ran and tried to stab Quincy.

Quincy dodged him and ran toward the hearth. He picked up another of the iron bludgeons, his mind racing.

Get out, he thought. *Just get out and go to Amelia.*

He tried to bolt for the door, but Dr. Seward stopped him. He swung the poker in a wide arc and missed Quincy by a hair. Seward quickly regained his momentum and swung again.

This time the poker collided with Quincy's, and Quincy felt the reverberation travel up his arm, sending shock waves of pain through him. It was all he could do to throw Seward back.

"Why did you kill those women?" shouted Quincy, hoping to distract Seward.

Seward scoffed. "As if they were worthy to live. Whores, the lot of them. When my master tired of them, not needing them for his purpose, I disposed of them. They were only prostitutes, not fit to walk the earth." He lunged, driving the poker forward.

Quincy blocked it and tried to run around the table. Quincy pushed the table over, trying to knock Seward over.

Seward dodged the onslaught of medical instruments, glass bottles, and papers that came flying toward him. Quincy realized that Seward only needed one good blow to his skull to crush it.

How in the hell am I going to get out?

As Seward regained his footing after the table, he grinned at Quincy. "You cannot escape," he said. "And I shall greatly enjoy killing you."

Quincy's eyes darted around the room. He knew that Seward felt what he himself had felt so many times before: the thrill of the hunt, the feeling of power as one's prey cowered, the absolute confidence of what would happen next.

Which is why Quincy did the unexpected.

No hunter ever expected one's prey to leap toward him, but that was exactly what Quincy did.

With a great yell, Quincy charged and hurled into Dr. Seward's middle, tackling him, like the players of the new game of football. They both fell back, and the poker flew from Seward's hand.

In one fluid motion, Quincy grabbed the knife hidden in his boot and stabbed Dr. Seward in the heart.

You're wrong, Amelia, he thought grimly. *I'm capable of far worse than I ever thought.*

Dr. Seward gasped and went still. He began to gurgle helplessly.

"You think that you will save her, the female? You think that you can stop my master?" said Seward, as his blood began to pool around him. "We are bound together, him and I. Whatever I think, he knows. He bound me to him mentally. He gives me visions, and I give him messages." Seward gasped again, using the last of his strength to whisper his last few words. "Even now, I am sending him a warning. The villagers will protect him. You cannot defeat him."

Then suddenly, his eyes went blank, as a ribbon of blood trickled from his mouth.

Quincy stood over the body of Dr. Seward. "Perhaps you are right, old friend," he said. "But I can try."

Chapter 30

I couldn't breathe. Not the least reason because Quincy had betrayed me. It hurt more than I wanted it to. He had given this—this Lucy his blood. Blood that should have been mine. That I wanted to be mine.

He's nothing more than a distraction, remember? I told myself savagely.

It had to be true. For if there were any alternative, if Quincy meant more to me than simply a passing tryst, two wanderers, then I don't think I could forgive him.

Perhaps he did not know what it meant, I thought. Perhaps he's just a stupid human, like all the rest of them.

Or maybe he could have thought. That's what I adored about him—that he was a human who thought, who didn't let the ways of his kind taint his ability to think for himself. Or at least, I had thought so.

As the miles passed beneath my feet, I tried not to think about what it all meant. As I ran toward the east, I ran away from what my heart wanted but my mind revolted against. Deep within, I wanted Quincy, needed him like I had needed nothing else in this world. Not Victor, not even blood.

What was it about him? His cavalier attitude, his breathtaking smile, the way that his fingers brushed the hilt of the knife as though he were caressing a lover, caressing me?

The cities turned into villages; buildings, churches, and libraries turned into rolling hills and uncultivated meadows; people who wore their wealth turned into peasants, who could barely scratch out an existence in the dirt. Somehow, the journey seemed so much shorter this time around. Why is that, with return journeys?

I listened for the scream of the wolves at night, tried to stuff my ears with mud, just to keep the savage voice in my head quiet. Nothing helped. Nothing could get the sickening sinking sensation out of my stomach.

Moonlight. A peasant's barn. I was close to my old home, the old castle, but it was no longer mine. I was an orphan now, caught between two places, unable to return to either of them. The sun was rising, as I jumped from the floor to the second story of the barn, where extra hay was kept. I lifted a horse blanket over my head, to stay hidden out of the sight of the humans. I would be gone by sundown.

In my stubbornness, I did not want to forgive him. And as I lay my head against a rough patch of straw, I did not realize that events would culminate into something I could have never anticipated.

Chapter 31

I was awoken by the harsh sound of the peasants speaking. It took my mind a few moments to adjust to the language. Whereas English had a sharpness to it, reminiscent of frozen lakes and barren landscapes, the patois of the villagers sounded as though it were carved from the mountains themselves.

"They will arrive in a few hours. We must be ready to protect the master," said a man.

I was alert instantly.

"How do we know, father?"

"One is recognizable. The man with the white hair—"

Jonathan, I thought.

—He came here a few months ago, to visit the master. He is said to be in their group. They want to do the master harm. We must not let that happen."

"Understood, father."

"They are moving toward the castle. The master is still weak in his chest. We must protect him."

The duo left the barn, the door creaking shut behind them.

Quincy!

They must have left London and traveled without stopping, taking one of those infernal, screeching metal contraptions that I saw snake its way through the country. Even though I had vampiric speed, I could not travel during the day, as they could.

Even as I was bolting upright and jumping down to the ground, I realized that Victor must have enchanted the villagers or mesmerized them or used some untapped vampiric power that I did not know we had. They spoke of unswerving loyalty, yet who is loyal to a monster? I knew that some of the villagers gossiped about us, cast terrified glances toward the castle and made Christian signs of protection against it.

Yet these peasants were willing to die for Victor.

And so, heart in my mouth, I set off down the road to find Victor, to find Quincy.

I was not sure who I wanted to kill more.

THE MOON WAS COMPLETELY risen when I saw the carriage come around a bend in the earth. It was racing, the horses nearly falling all over themselves. It lurched on its huge axels, spitting dirt from the back wheels.

Quincy stood in the road, and my heart raged and thrilled to see him. I wanted to hurt him. I wanted to kiss him. There was so much left unspoken between us, so much that we still needed to say, that I needed to stay. All I really wanted was closure. Wasn't it? Did I not want to be free of these ghastly chains forever, to no longer be in thrall to the colossal burden of love?

I had no time to think about such things. Everyone was prepared to fight.

Victor was inside his coffin in the carriage. He had been severely injured, and he needed to be placed deep within the earth of his birthplace. I knew that he had communicated all of this to the villagers.

Quincy and the others stood, blocking the path, torches in hand. There were five of them.

Five, against dozens of villagers.

They had guns against the rudimentary tools of the peasants: pitchforks, axes, some knives. However, this ragtag little group was held back by their desire to not shed human blood, to kill no one. They were motivated to protect the sanctity of human life.

The villagers had no such compunction.

Victor's orders controlled them completely: mow down anyone who stands between them and the castle.

But, I felt a dawning horror as I read the minds of the humans. Not all of them were here to protect Victor. Some of them were pretending to go, in disguise as those who wanted to see the master restored to his rightful castle. Victor was weak and could not control everyone. Quincy and the others had convinced several to charge the castle and destroy it.

And all who lived there.

My sisters.

This will be chaos, I thought.

As much as I wanted to protect Quincy, protect Victor (and yet, somehow, kill them both), I knew there were two other beings who I would never want to see dead, and they were Catherine and Berenice. I felt as though I were being torn in half, but I knew I had to protect them. I had to warn them.

And so, regretting it infinitely later, I ran away from the fight.

Chapter 32

Quincy stood, with his heart in his mouth. The villagers were gathering all around them, some breaking away to storm the castle. It was madness; he could not tell who was on his side and who was not, who wanted to protect the infamous count, and who was even know tearing down the bricks to get at his three women.

The demon women, they all whispered. He had heart it countless times as he had wound his way through the mountains by train, then by carriage when the terrain became too rugged.

Now, he stared down the villagers, the smoke from their torches making his eyes water. He gripped his knife tighter. He just needed to plunge the knife into the count's heart.

But he was inside his carriage surrounded by dozens of villagers.

There was a horrible moment, when the earth seemed to stand still. Quincy and his group stared down the villagers, who, true to Dr. Seward's word, had raced to protect their master. It was some dark and evil magic, but the why of it was not important right now. The only thing of importance was how sharp their rusty pitchforks looked. As sharp as their eyes, which peered into the deepening night. No one moved. No one dared to breath.

Then, they attacked.

It was as if a dam broke; they came screaming toward the group, weapons raised.

Van Helsing fired a warning shot into the air, but the villagers advanced. One raised his weapon and was about to swing it down onto Quincy's skull.

Quincy blocked, pivoted, and drove the weapon out of the villager's hand. Still, the man advanced, with a wild look in his eyes. He was going to fight Quincy, even weaponless.

Quincy managed to shove him away, only to encounter another villager. The ax came furiously toward him.

He blocked the swing of his ax with the knife, feeling the impact travel up his arm. He punched the man so hard that he dropped, unconscious, to the ground.

Looking around wildly, Quincy realized that there were too many villagers to fight off. Van Helsing was struggling mightily with a woman who was trying to scratch his eyes out. Mina was fighting off a villager twice her size with a staff.

"Quincy! We will have to shoot!" she screamed.

"No!" cried Van Helsing. "The only one to die is the vampire!"

"What about us?" Mina kicked a villager in the stomach, her dress swinging wildly. "What of our lives?"

There was no way to outfight them. He would have to make a wild attempt to kill the count.

Then, in the midst of the fighting, a cool, clear voice came into his head. It was a voice that he wished he spend all his life listening to. It belonged to the one being he wanted to see above all others, the one who he wished he could apologize to, for whatever it was that he did.

We can be destroyed by fire.

Quincy swung his knife at an oncoming villager. He dodged out of the way, but not before the knife sliced part of his side. The wound was not deep, but the villager howled anyway.

That gave him just enough time to reach into his pocket and pull out a box of matches. He ran straight toward the wagon, striking three matches against the strip, watching hope bloom like the flame.

Flinging the matches through the open window, he watched as the carriage began to catch fire. Quincy sliced the harness that held the horses, and they galloped away.

The villagers, panicked, began to break into the carriage to pull out the count's coffin. However, only the hardiest ones tried. Upon seeing the raging flames, many of the villagers ran away, not risking themselves to the fire.

Van Helsing and the others managed to beat back what few villagers remained, driving them into the forest.

The coffin now lay on the ground, and Quincy was surprised to see how small it looked. He smashed the lock and threw open the cover. There lay the count, now stirring. He was pale, much paler than his normal hue. The poisoned silver was working through his veins, and he could barely lift a hand.

Quincy pulled his knife, the same one that Amelia had given him.

He thought of her as he plunged the knife into the count's chest. As he ripped it free, he made sure to sever the head from its neck.

Quincy made one fatal error though, despite all his years of hunting. He allowed emotion to rule him, allowed a singular rage to enter into him. This was the being that had tormented Amelia and her sisters all these years. This was the origin of so much pain and suffering, and Quincy had a savage glee in seeing the light fade from the count's eyes.

It was only a moment. But it was enough for a rogue villager to sneak behind the carriage and stab Quincy in the side.

Chapter 33

I doubled around the castle, finding a secret entrance. The villagers were running after me, waving their torches into the air. I could take out five, easily, and maybe even fend off ten, but twenty? Fifty?

Even vampires have their limit.

Still, I ran. Throwing open the door, I did not bother to check behind me to see if it was closed. For all their anger at being terrorized over the years, they would find some way to break into the castle.

What madness. Normally, I would have happily reveled in the utter chaos of humans running around trying to destroy everything in their path, but just then, I could not. I had to warn my sisters. Even now, the voices of the villagers echoed against the stone walls. Angry, riotous. They wanted blood as much as we did.

I flew from room to room, looking for Catherine and Berenice. Nowhere. My heart sped up as I realized that I might not find them in time.

Running up the steps, someone shouted, "Over there! There's a staircase!"

"Get them!"

"Get the demon women!"

Damn!

I ran to the top floor. Surely, they must have heard the commotion.

They were too wrapped up in their affairs. Berenice was by the fire, reading, and Catherine was tossing knives into the wall at a framed picture of some human or other. When I burst into the room, they glanced up sharply.

"Amelia!" gasped Berenice. "Where—"

"No time," I said, striding to the window. Glancing out, I saw dozens more villagers pour into the castle. Some of them were fighting each other, as they realized that some wanted to protect the count and some wanted to destroy him. It was a battleground out there, and I saw the flash of Quincy's form as he fought off attackers.

I should be protecting him, I thought. Soon.

"They are coming." I turned to face them. "We have to leave. Now."

"Who, the village folk?" said Catherine scornfully. "We can crush them like gnats."

"Not dozens of them. They bring fire and silver," I said.

Only then did fear cross both my sister's faces. I grabbed their hands and began to pull them to the door.

"Where—"

The door flew open. The faces of the villagers, twisted in fury were the first things that we saw.

"Follow my lead," I said. My voice was pitched so quietly that only they could hear it. Then, in a louder tone, I said, "Oh thank goodness you've come!"

I ran and threw myself at my would-be attacker's feet.

The villagers piled into the room, all bearing huge torches. The scorching heat reached across the room and caressed my face. I could feel it even from dozens of feet away.

At hearing my words, the villagers looked confused.

"Where are the devil women?" one demanded. He looked as though he had not showered in a week. Smelled like it too.

I looked up at him, hoping that my real fear masked my deceit. "They have kept us prisoner for so long! And now you have rescued us!"

I glanced behind me and gave my sisters a pointed look.

Berenice was the first to react. "Yes, thank you! You have saved us from the monstrous, wicked women!"

I swore I could hear the sarcasm in Catherine's voice as she said, "Yes, the completely wicked women who held us hostage." Thankfully, the villagers did not note her irony.

"Who are you?" the large, smelly one demanded.

I looked up at him, making my eyes as wide as the moon. "We were visiting dignitaries. Our husbands wanted to purchase land from the count, but he...he...dispatched them!" I covered my face in the man's pants and pretended to weep.

My sisters flung themselves at the feet of the villagers as well.

"And the women?"

I shrugged and sighed helplessly. "Driven off by others who came before you. They had locked us in this room. Now you have saved us!" And I began to kiss the man's feet. I wanted to retch, but if it meant my sisters' survival, I could bear a peasant's smelly foot.

The villager, perhaps unused to this sort of action from a woman of aristocratic birth, was clearly uncomfortable.

"Well then," he mumbled, slowly moving his foot away from my kissing lips. "Then you are free. We will—we go." He jerked his head at the others and they left.

When they had shut the door, I breathed in relief.

"I cannot believe you kissed that man's foot," said Catherine. "How disgusting. How repulsive. How—"

"Yes, but we are alive, my beautiful, haughty sister," I said, returning to the window. Most of the peasants had suddenly left.

The next thing I saw was someone stabbing Quincy.

Chapter 34

My breath seemed to leave my body. In that instant, I understood that I wanted Quincy more than anything. Perhaps he didn't know about the blood bond. Perhaps it shouldn't have mattered so much to me.

I flew down the castle, now reassured that my sisters were safe.

Running across the lawn, I looked into the frightened faces of Jonathan, Mina, and Van Helsing. The one called Arthur Holmwood was panting, his hands on his knees.

"Where is he?" I demanded.

The others stood silently, looking at each other. I could feel the faint rays of the sun as they were coming over the edge of the earth. Already, my eyelids were pushing down, wanting to close, and my skin tingled from the first burns the sun inflicted.

"Where is he?" I repeated, half-mad with desperation.

They parted, and Quincy lay on the ground, dark blood pooled around him, soaking into the earth. I ran to his side, moving so quickly that the others saw only a blur.

"What happened?" I demanded of Jonathan, turning to face him. Mina looked white and sad, holding back tears. Van Helsing hobbled a bit on a wounded leg.

He motioned to Quincy and said, "He delivered the death blow. He stabbed the Count in the heart. He is dead, but one of the villagers stabbed him with a knife." Jonathan did not look like he would be able to stand on his feet much longer. Our ragged little party had been nearly torn to bits.

"Where is that villager?" I demanded. I would rip his heart out myself.

Jonathan shook his head. "Gone. I dispatched him."

Good.

My mind processed the shock of Victor's death. It was like a thousand iron chains around my heart had suddenly disappeared. I felt light, dizzy, and overcome. A part of me mourned his loss, mourned the fact that I would never see him or hear him again. To think that all our memories were only that now—memories. There was no more man to tie them to me.

Yet surprisingly, I did not really miss him. I had lived in fear all my life that if he were gone, I would not be able to live without him. I feared missing him so much that I had never let him go, had never realized how poisonous he had been to my soul. And yet now that he was gone, it only felt as though I had shorn my hair or lost a tooth: a bit shocking at first, but only made me lighter.

Quincy gasped, choking on the blood. "Amelia", he said, "I love..."

"Quiet," I commanded. "Do not speak. Concentrate on fighting with every ounce of energy you possess."

His breathing was ragged and came in spurts. I felt tears sting my eyes. Every second speeded us toward his death, and I could not imagine losing him. His death would create a hole in me that I would never recover from. My mind rattled through options and plans, but none of them stuck.

Glancing over his body, I saw the gaping wounds in his side. Part of me was surprised that he was not already dead. To my shame, my vampire nature wanted to gently lap his blood, even now. I quickly throttled the urge inside and forced myself to concentrate on saving him.

He began to close his eyes, and I slapped his face. "Do not leave me," I said. "You are forbidden to do so."

A faint smile played on his lips until it was replaced by a grimace of pain.

"It will be worth it, for you," he said. "Now you are free."

Free yes, but what was freedom without him? What did I gain if I could not love this man every second of every day for the rest of my immortal life? He was the one who freed me. He had delivered the death blow to my vicious torment. Was I just going to do nothing?

I could not believe it. All my vampiric life I had believed that I had needed Victor to live, to survive. It was simply lust and fear I felt, not real love. I had thought that I had a family with him, that I had fulfillment in our relationship, but it was built on lies and manipulation. He had twisted the truth so many times that my vision had become skewed. But now...now I knew what real love felt like, and Quincy had shown me. He had shown me patience and selflessness.

When I thought of Quincy, I felt warm and happy, but savage like I did with Victor. I felt like I wanted to give him the best parts of myself, to love him with the ardor that he deserved. I loved him because he lifted me up instead of tearing me to pieces. He looked past my innumerable faults and loved me despite myself. Looking down at this rough, American man, I wanted to pour whatever life remained in me into him.

"If you die, I will not live," I said. But what could be done? I was no doctor, and the closest one was twenty miles away. Even with my vampire speed, I could not go to the village, find him, and bring him back before Quincy departed into death.

His eyelids fluttered and what remained of my shattered heart clenched. His heartbeat was becoming weaker.

I let out a scream, a primal animal howl, and the others had to cover their ears to avoid their eardrums shattering.

I would give you my own life if I could, I thought. *I would give it to your right now.*

Something in me began to click. Victor had always been a liar. I saw that now. He had lied about leaving the country. I had left the deep forests and mountains of Transylvania and had not died. He had lied about our maker's bond. So why not about being able to make another vampire?

My mind began to race, clutching onto the hope like a mother bear seizing her bear cubs.

Can I do it? I thought. *It is possible?*

He was going to die. I did not want to risk his last few moments, speeding him toward the infinite black, but I had to try. My mind pushed past the fear of failure; I had no idea how to create another vampire, and Victor had never told me how, but I needed to attempt it. There was no other way.

I remembered the way that my heart had beat so softly when Victor changed me. Leaning over his neck, my fangs extended, and I whispered, "I love you," into his ear. I bit into him, feeling the enchanting and heady sensation of drinking human blood, but I did not do it for pleasure. If I had done one thing in my life unselfishly, this was it. With each draught, I prayed to any god that would hear me to spare him. I hated that I drawing him closer to death, when I was trying to avoid sending him over the edge. His eyes fluttered and closed with the sensation, and I knew, even if he died, he would go without pain. Blood tears fell from my eyes, mixing with his blood, as I drank from my darling.

I could feel it, the point of death coming close. I had no idea what I was doing, and I reviled myself for believing Victor all those years.

"Stay with me," I whispered. "Stay with me through the years and love me. Love me as I love you."

He cracked open his eyes, and I could imagine how difficult it must be for him to do such a tiny gesture. I, too, had once been on the verge of death.

"I promise," he whispered.

"Forever?" I asked.

He looked into my eyes, and I saw the infinite. I knew that he was on the edge of a great precipice, and one word would send him over the edge. He had a choice between two infinities, two darknesses: one of everlasting sleep, where the black obscurity of death would rein and he would have no more trouble or feel pain; the other of life eternal, cursed to the darkness of night. Quincy gave a short, sweet nod.

"Forever," he promised.

And I knew that he was brave enough to face this dark road. I knew this man, who had stared at death in the form of a lion and did not shake. Whatever might come, I knew that Quincy and I would be able to face it together.

Releasing my teeth from his neck, I bit into my wrist, the same way that I had seen Victor bite into his all those centuries ago. My blood flowed, and I cradled his head into mine. I lifted his head so that he could more easily drink. Unlike when I turned, this choice was his. I knew what it was to live with this damnation, and I prayed that Quincy would one day forgive me, but I could not let him go. I loved him too much.

"Then drink," I said, and he latched onto my wrist. I could feel the stares of the others, watching and wondering what would happen. Out of the corner of my eye, I saw my sisters flee to the castle crypt. Because they were not as old as I was, they could not stand the rising sun for as long as I could.

As he drank, I felt with each pull a pressure growing in my body, a delicious, throbbing sensation, and I knew that he was close to transforming. He drank, and I felt his heart stop. He shuddered and convulsed, and I realized that he was dying, just as I had died. Still, he kept drinking from me, and I felt my body release in the same pleasurable climax he must have felt then. Our bodies tangled as our hearts became one.

When neither of us could take any more, he stopped, falling back toward the ground. I felt momentarily weakened, as he had taken nearly all of my blood. Some sensible part of me told myself that I would have to feed, and feed soon, to replenish my store.

But that did not matter.

Did it work? I wondered. *Did I do enough?* The fear that I had lost him forever made me squeeze my eyes shut.

I glanced over to him and saw that his wound was healing quickly, his flesh stitching itself back together. Relief coursed through my body, and I began to laugh. Even the others visibly relaxed at seeing their companion revive. It seemed that there was no other greater sight than that, of his body shaking off the shackles of death.

In all my long life, I did not feel happier than I did in that moment. I wanted to run and shout for joy, but all I could manage was to roll over closer to him. He wrapped his wonderfully strong arms around me, and for an instant, I thought that it would all be ripped away from me, that it was a horrible dream and that I would wake up and he would be gone.

It was no dream. My heart rose and I felt that I might explode from sheer joy. We had made it. He and I had chosen to be together. After everything, we would live as one in the blood.

He opened his eyes, and I saw the characteristic flash of red. He was a vampire. He had crossed over the threshold of death and yet he lived. He had so much to learn, so much yet that he still did not understand. But I would be there, guiding him through all of it.

Leaning over to kiss my forehead, he whispered, "Forever," and I knew that he meant it. Whatever the rages and ravages of time, whatever problem might spring out like a lion from its den, whatever silly or petty argument we might have, I knew that we would face it together. I felt such relief at his life that my chest ached with it.

He looked down at himself, at his hands, and his eyes held a childlike fascination with everything, just as I knew mine had. I let him be immersed in the new feelings, the new sensations. I wanted to wrap myself around him, lock his lips to mine, but I knew there would be time. There would always be time now.

We stood up together. As the sun came up, Quincy held up a hand, shielding himself from the sun.

"We must run," I whispered. "Day is upon us. I promise I will explain everything. But we need to hurry."

Grabbing his hand, I pulled him toward the castle, and we ran toward the crypt.

Chapter 35

The moon rose full and bloody, an orange globe in the sky, as Quincy and I rose to take our places along the dark road that had chosen us. I squeezed his hand tightly, simply feeling the weight of it, the delicious physicality. He and I would have so much to talk about, so many years to discuss our deepest dreams and desires, our hopes and secret yearnings, but for now, it was enough to simply stand on the cobbled road outside the castle. But soon, Quincy's inner nature took hold, and he wanted to explore. We began to stroll around the deep, dark forests that I loved so much, the rugged mountains always keeping watch over us in the distance.

He kept looking about, and I could not help but smile as he seemed so much like a child caught in the wonder of something new. My heart gave a surge, for I realized that I had been missing that feeling, of awe, of discovering something trivial with new eyes and finding it extraordinary.

Before we had walked out into the night, we had made love quickly, voraciously; then, satiated in the knowledge that we were alive, we did it again, slowly, languidly, with all the time that our now immortal lives had at our disposal.

As we walked, I did not speak of Victor, and Quincy never again mentioned his name. We did not have to. I was free of the chains that had for so long wrapped around my heart. There was no need for jealousy or rivalry; even if Victor had survived, there would be no need for any of that. I belonged to Quincy, body and soul, mind and heart.

"Well, what now?" asked Quincy.

"What do you mean?"

I was simply content to let this moment wash over me, the crush of pine needles beneath our feet sending up their sweet, sticky aroma, and the call of owls deep in the trees echoing my own hunting instincts.

"Where would you like to live?" he asked.

I turned to him, my arm threaded through his, a cocked eyebrow silently asking him to explain and a smile playing on my lips.

"Anywhere, as long as it is with you," I answered, completely sincere. I would follow him to the ends of the earth.

"Yes, yes, that's all well and good," Quincy replied, his seriousness hiding the playful sarcasm beneath. "But would you not like to stay here, in your beautiful castle?" He then gestured behind us, to the towering walls, the imposing turrets, and the graceful arches that had stood for centuries. My home.

Except, I realized, it was no longer my home. It was simply a shell that had housed me for many years. My elegant prison of stone.

"No," I replied. "I would rather go elsewhere."

"Where? We can go anywhere, as you said. Tell me, and we'll go. We could go to the lush South American continent. Or the hot jungles of exotic India. Or the cool steppes of the far north. I could even take you to Texas, the place of my birth. Only name a place, and we will make it ours."

I thought. It was a bit amusing to me, that Quincy's first concern would be where we would live. I thought of a globe, spinning on its axis, the world at my fingertips now. I had been shut in for so long that the options seemed overwhelming at first. I closed my eyes, dizzy with all the grand possibilities that awaited Quincy and me. There was so much to explore, so much beauty and wonder in the world to behold.

Then, I opened my eyes, sure of my decision.

"London," I replied. "I would like to live in London."

I admit, its filthy streets and grimy people had somehow stolen my heart. I loved all its nooks and crannies, its gray skies, ever-present rain, and bustling energy. It had a pulse to it that my dear countryside had never known. Every day was like a heartbeat, and its people were the brilliant blood that kept it alive.

Quincy nodded once. "London it is." And then he kissed me deeply, as though sealing his promise with his scorching kiss.

"We can always move again, if we tire of it," I said, positive that I would never tire of its charm, its quaint people, cultivated gardens, and electric streetlights.

"That we can."

Suddenly, I turned to him. There was something that I needed to do immediately; I felt as though I had stumbled onto the most wonderful treasure in the world, and I longed to show that treasure to the people who mean the most to me.

"Come," I said, pulling him back in the direction of the castle.

I took Quincy to meet my sisters, the people most important to me than anyone else in the world, save Quincy. At first, I felt the sting of guilt for having left them without a word, without writing during the weeks I had been away.

"Shame on you," said Berenice, throwing her arms around me. "We were sure that you were dead."

"We are all dead, are we not?" asked Quincy sincerely, his brow furrowing.

"Finally dead, then. All dead," replied Berenice. "And who is this?"

She and Catherine instinctively drew together, our tribal bonds unconsciously coming out in every action. Their teeth gleamed in the pale moonlight, but Quincy no longer feared them, as he once might have. Perhaps now, he felt a different sort of fear, the kind where he did not want to offend them and risk disappointing me. This was my family, and Quincy was hyper-conscious of the gravity of this meeting, from the way he kept his back ramrod straight, to the bobbing of his throat.

And I introduced Quincy to them. We took a seat in the large, living area, a fire crackling in the background, sharpening my words as I told them everything that had transpired since I had left and now returned, the prodigal sister. I told them of tracking the murderer in London, of Quincy's discovery, of finding Victor's newest target and dispatching her.

"But the boundary," said Catherine, the youngest of us. "How did you cross it?"

"Victor lied; there is no boundary. We are free to roam as we wish."

Catherine sucked in her breath sharply. She had never found confinement easy, as I had in some years. She had railed against it, fighting it with every ounce of strength, unlike Berenice or I, who had come to accept imprisonment through years of Victor's manipulations.

I also told them of our plans to live in London, when suddenly, a thought struck me.

"Come with us," I said. "Live in London."

I turned to Quincy, my eyes, silently earnest. "You do not mind, do you?"

My two sisters flicked their eyes toward Quincy, as if their entire opinion of him hinged on his response, which it most likely did.

"Of course," he said. "I am the newcomer to this family."

Catherine jumped up from her seat, and immediately ran from the room. When she was in her own private chamber, she shouted down to us, certain that we could all hear with our vampiric ears, "I am packing. When do we leave?"

"As soon as possible," I said, eager to begin my new life with Quincy. Life had never seemed so full of promise and expectation as it did then, so ripe with possibilities. I could go anywhere, do anything. I leaned over and kissed Quincy full on the mouth, too happy to do anything else.

It was a strange feeling, happiness, as though I had drank Victor's finest champagne, feeling the tiny bubbles burst within. It was sparking, electrical. I was drunk on Quincy, and it was scarcely our first night together.

We left the following night. Quincy explained to Jonathan, Van Helsing, and the others about his transformation, about us. Then, Van Helsing requested a meeting with us. We were as all shocked as one might expect us to be, a human requesting the audience of a vampire. However, I agreed, because Quincy was now my husband in everything but name, and my sisters agreed, because I was the eldest.

We met on the steps of the lawn, the moon rising behind the castle. Stars were beginning to poke out into the night, bringing an elegance the day, with all its brutal heat, could never have.

All of the humans were wound as tightly as coiled springs. Jonathan's face was pale, and he looked as though he might faint at any moment; Mina must have been the stronger of the two, for she frowned when we approached, but managed to make her knees not shake, as Jonathan's did. Indeed, I thought Mina would make an excellent vampire, and I briefly fantasized about making her one of us. However, with the addition of Quincy, one more was enough for now.

Arthur Holmwood looked as though he wanted to cower in some dark corner. He kept grabbing the stake at his side, but I knew that he would not be able to raise it in time if any one of us decided to strike.

My sisters poorly concealed their contempt for the humans. I suppose I could not blame them; I, too, still thought of humans as something...less than vampire, but I hoped that would change with time. The tension between our two groups was thick, making the air seem heavier than it really was. Even though a cool breeze stirred the edges of our dresses and made our hair swish across our faces, it seemed as though the world hung thick and still around us.

Van Helsing stood before the group, his arms crossed. For all his bravado, his heart still began to accelerate when we approached.

"So you wish to return to London," he said, his voice sharp.

"Yes," I replied, slightly amused at this human and his antics. Then, I chided myself for adopting an attitude of superiority toward the human. I suppose I could not laugh and scoff so much at humans anymore; I had fallen in love with one. "I would like to call London my home."

"To stay there, we have conditions."

"Conditions?" laughed Catherine, the scorn apparent in her voice. "Such as?"

"Such as you may not kill a single human in the city, or anywhere. You may not kill another human ever again," he replied. He casually laid a hand on the sharpened blade by his side.

"What if I kill a human right now?" said Catherine smoothly, as she stepped toward Van Helsing.

I threw an arm out to stop her.

"These restrictions are a bit harsh for us at the current moment—" I began.

"Or any moment whatsoever," muttered Catherine.

"Can there not be a compromise?" I finished.

"Compromise? *Compromise?*" said Van Helsing. "Compromise when human life is at stake? I think not."

"Some of us have been used to killing and feeding on humans for centuries," I said, grinning, letting Van Helsing see my sharp incisors.

Jonathan gulped.

"So there may be a small...adjustment phase."

Van Helsing looked as though he smelled something rotten.

"Innocent lives cannot be taken by—by fiends. By *monsters*," he said.

"And there is where I think we may have our compromise," I replied. "You are concerned with innocent life. We could debate for ages on end about what constitutes 'innocent,' but I think that we can agree that a human who takes another human's life is not innocent."

Van Helsing nodded slowly, as though he were walking into a trap. His eyes narrowed into slits, his hand still clenched around the sharpened stake.

I glanced to Quincy, the man I was now deeply and completely in love with. He had given me the idea, the beautiful soul.

"Men like this Dr. Seward have existed in all ages, at all times," I said, taking a step toward the group of humans. "They have always killed, for no other reason than the pleasure of it. Or thieves slit a throat for a quick chance at a gold coin."

Everyone tensed at my approach. Mina even threw an arm around Jonathan, not for her protection but his.

"What if we make those humans the targets of our nightly needs?" I said. "In this way, no innocent blood is shed. And we rid the streets of those who you would also like to see gone."

Van Helsing hesitated but I could see the acceptance in his eyes. "Murder is still murder," he said, refusing to accept too quickly.

"Yes, but it will prevent more than what would have happened," I said, now face to face with Van Helsing. "Don't be tedious."

"She does have a point," whispered Jonathan.

"Indeed..." trailed Van Helsing. He looked at me and my three sisters and Quincy's changed face. He was now more handsome, if it could be believed, all traces of the human slowly vanishing. He no longer had the fine wrinkles that had studded his mouth and eyes, and the dark transition into vampire had made his hair shinier and thicker and had given his eyes an eerie, preternatural glow.

"Fine," he agreed.

I reached out my hand to shake, and he hesitated before he took it. However, in the end, the promise of fewer murderers on the streets of London was too good to resist.

I turned to Catherine and Berenice. "Satisfied?"

"Not remotely," said Catherine, but she flew to the castle to collect her things at any rate.

Berenice smiled, her best attempt to quell the fears of the group of humans, but she still must have looked terrifying to them. "Don't mind her; she is young and impetuous." She turned her beautiful head to Van Helsing and said, "Having restrictions will take some time to become accustomed to them, but if it means leaving this place..." And here she gazed at the castle. "Then we'll accommodate them."

Chapter 36

And so, we left. We said goodbye to the castle, possibly forever, but as my sisters and I knew, forever was quite a long time, and things had a way of appearing down the road. Things that you thought you would never see again mysteriously and inexplicably showed up in your life, against all possibility.

As we traveled overland back to London, I showed Quincy the mystery of our way of being. He took to it as naturally as one could. It was as though all his life was simply a precursor to becoming a vampire. His hunter's instincts were deadly and keen, and I loved how he was able to transition to the dark nature of a vampire so easily. We stuck to dark roads, deep forests where thieves roamed. We always gave them a chance, to prove that they did not have murder in their hearts; however, as soon as their blades flashed in the moonlight, severing another human's bond with life, that was when we struck. We cleaned up the roads from our rugged Carpathian Mountains, all the way to the waters of the Thames.

I loved watching the expressions on my sisters' faces change each time they came upon some new delight, some wonder of the earth. The world had changed so much since our imprisonment, and it seemed that so had we. We had not realized it at the time, of course, but we had, slowly and steadily, as a glacier moves across the wide, frigid seas.

True to our word, we did not kill another innocent being, and we kept the peace with Van Helsing. We settled into London, loving the quick pace, and as time went on, the speed of life only increased. Horse-drawn carriages turned into motor cars; electric lights replaced gas lamps; soon we had these fabulous machines called computers, then a strange, wonderful ether called the internet. As time flowed on, we continued to hone our skills as hunters and killers, but for a higher purpose. At least, for a purpose justifiable to let us stay in London.

Even after Van Helsing died, when he finally laid his weary, proud head to rest, we continued to honor our agreement. I could not have said why, exactly, but for me, Quincy had a lot to do with it. I shrunk from the thought more and more of killing innocent humans, especially since I had loved one and who had helped me see that there was another way to live. In time, I even thought humans were kind of cute, in their fragile way, like a baby bunny or helpless kitten. There were others who were far more sinister, who took without feeling. I used to be one of those beings, but Quincy gave me a second chance.

Catherine needed the most adjustment, and she had a few…shall we say 'accidents' when she went too far and could not control herself. These we did not mention to Van Helsing.

And Quincy? He learned to adjust to being a vampire.

But that is another story.

Epilogue

I walked into the flat, letting the sounds of honking traffic drift away from me. The television was on, although no one was watching it, which drove me crazy. I was still distrustful of the talking boxes; Berenice was crazy about them.

Someone grabbed me from behind in a bear hug. Smelling the cologne I had bought Quincy for Christmas, I nuzzled into him.

He kissed the top of my head. "How did it go?" he asked.

"The Sixth Precinct Killer will not be severing heads any longer," I said. "I gave him a batty-fang."

"Amelia, no one says that anymore," said Catherine, breezing into the room, with Berenice trailing behind her. "You'll blow our cover if you keep talking like some Victorian street urchin."

"Can I help it if the Victorians had some remarkably adept phrases?" I teased, taking off my coat and unholstering the guns at my sides. "We will need to re-stock soon. We're running out of ammunition."

"As I reminded you at least a month ago," said Catherine, flopping on the couch. "Can I take the next target? I'm getting...antsy." Catherine smiled, showing her fangs.

Suddenly, the black phone in the kitchen rang. We all had cell phones now. There was only one reason that phone ever rang.

I picked it up and held it out to Catherine. "Then this call is for you."

Thank you!

If you liked this book, there are ways that you can show your appreciation:

To sign up for my email list: http://eepurl.com/iqnA6s (THIS IS THE MOST IMPORTANT STEP YOU CAN TAKE!)

To leave a review on Amazon:

To support me on Patreon: https://lnkd.in/gerrmHj2

To support me in general: https://gofund.me/e003a267

Don't miss out!

Visit the website below and you can sign up to receive emails whenever Ariel Slick publishes a new book. There's no charge and no obligation.

https://books2read.com/r/B-A-UHPQ-TRSUC

BOOKS 2 READ

Connecting independent readers to independent writers.

Also by Ariel Slick

Royals of Sea and Song
Dracula's Women

Watch for more at https://www.slickwriting.com.

About the Author

Ariel Slick is an author and world traveler. Before she started writing full time, she received her Master of Library Science from Texas Woman's University. Although a Texas native, she dreamed of exchanging a sea of Indian paintbrushes for the turquoise of the Caribbean Sea, so she moved to the Dominican Republic. Now she lives in Texas where she writes full-time, when she's not taking care of her two adorable cats, inhaling books on lucid dreaming, or making cappuccinos. She is the co-author of the Good Harbor Witches Mystery series.

Read more at https://www.slickwriting.com.